Someone Always Robs the Poor

*for Bert McIntosh
from one warmer
to another.*

Carl

2 iii 17

Someone Always Robs
the Poor

Carl MacDougall

**FREIGHT
BOOKS**

First published 2017

Freight Books
49–53 Virginia Street
Glasgow, G1 1TS
www.freightbooks.co.uk

A CIP catalogue reference for this book is available from the British
Library.

ISBN 978-1-911332-13-8
eISBN 978-1-911332-14-5

Typeset by Freight in Plantin
Printed and bound by Bell and Bain, Glasgow

the publisher acknowledges investment from
Creative Scotland toward the publication of this book

For John Bampton (1939-2014)

Contents

Is this the place you now call home?

When they took the road into the hills, Deegan gathered his luggage and kept his hand on the case till the taxi stopped.

The driver hadn't spoken, but when he told him the fare, Deegan recognised the voice.

Donald?

The driver nodded.

Are you Donnie Robertson?

Aye. So is this you back?

Just for a visit. Are you still working at the fish farm?

There's your change.

Deegan had given him a two pound tip; too much, but he'd been silly. His mother told him the fish farm and the cement factory had closed along with the milk place where Lorna used to work making butter and a bit cheese. And Donda Robertson wouldn't be driving a taxi if he was still at the fish farm.

His mother was at the door, smaller than he remembered, thinner, and her clothes didn't fit.

She stretched her arms up towards him as he approached and held him without moving, her face in his clothes. Her hair needed washing and her make-up smudged his shirt. She held on to the wall as she moved from the door to the sitting room.

Lorna was in the scullery, drying her hands on a dish towel. She was almost two years older and more like a brother.

I'd go and talk to her, if I were you, I think you could do quite well there, she had told him more than once, when shyness left him standing.

I put the kettle on when I heard the taxi, she said, taking his coat into the lobby.

It was Donnie Robertson.

Is that what he's doing?

Strange, he'd have gone without speaking.

He always was a moody bugger. He was staying with that Lorraine McKay and her kids, one of them might even have been his, then she threw him out and Colin Robertson moved in.

And the fish farm closed?

Yeah, but not before he got the sack for stealing fish and trying to sell them in the pub.

So, life is pretty much the same?

Lorna smiled. I thought we might take a walk up by the loch when you've eaten, she said, putting down a plate of ham salad and chips, their mother's favourite meal.

Their eyes met and a smile skipped across her face as she went outside to phone.

His mother sat opposite, watching him eat, smiling when he looked up at her.

You were hungry, she said when she took his plate.

You didn't eat much.

I had plenty to eat earlier.

She said she was keeping well, tired at times, and it took her a while to get roused in the morning, but she was fine once she was up and about. The minister drops round every week and people from the church are always calling in to see what she needs. She has a home help and goes shopping with Ann, her carer, down to the Co-op once or twice a week. They get a taxi there and back and sometimes have a cup of tea in that new place. She doesn't go out much at night. She gets tired. It's her age.

He cleared the table and watched television while his mother dozed. Lorna had put on the electric blanket, the bedside radio was tuned low and when they saw their mother settled they took the path up the side of the house to the top of the hill where the moor stretched beyond the loch to the line of blue and grey hills in the background.

She knows, Lorna said. The other day she told me she was

holding on to see you again. The visit would give her a boost and, God love her, she's been waiting at the window since she got up this morning. Some days she doesn't get out of bed. And she finds the children difficult. She never says, but they're too active, too noisy or just in the way. I ask if she wants to see them and she always says yes, of course. But they're too much for her.

When Lorna talked about the children, her voice changed. Her face softened and she sometimes closed her eyes as if remembering an incident, an expression or the sound of their voice, the ways they mispronounced words.

And how about you?

Fine, she said. Managing, getting by.

And David?

He's much the same.

Managing and getting by?

You know things aren't great.

You said.

The path was narrow, so Lorna led the way. They had walked here most weekends since childhood. This was where they shared their first secrets, had their first cigarettes and sexual explorations. Did you have a nice time last night? one would ask the other at Sunday lunch.

Lovely, thanks.

Where did you go?

We just had a walk down by the loch.

He was glad a wind had got up. It was how he remembered it, the rustle of birch leaves, the twisted hawthorns, the ruck of stones and slavers of mud at the end of the path.

They didn't speak, but sat where they always sat, watching the breeze cross the water.

I came down here the other day, Lorna said, when we knew you were coming, definitely coming this time. I must have been here for an hour or more, just sitting like this, staring over the water.

And from the bog beyond the loch a curlew cry, sharp and

3

insistent, made them smile.

Still here, he said.

Always, she said. Never leaves.

She reached across and put her hand on his hands. He turned and they smiled.

It's good to see you, she said.

I never thought I'd be back. I don't mean the house or the village, I mean here, with you and the curlews.

I never thought you'd be back. Mum says she'd like to see you settled, but that's as far as it goes. She never asks if you're over what happened, or if I think it would be okay for you to be here, if they'd somehow forgotten or decided to let things rest.

Is she around?

Still here and so is he, living up the back of the estate. She doesn't come out all that often and there's no sign that she's done anything but settle. I'm told she has to attend the hospital every two or three months, just to see things are as they should be, but that's as much as I know. He's still with the forestry.

And the wee one?

Don't. It will just upset you. She's a lovely, happy wee thing, bright and pretty. She's in Millie's class.

Does Millie know?

Of course not. But they're friendly. I don't know what I'll do if she asks if Lucy can come and play or stay the night.

Does Mum ever say?

Not to me. She knows it would upset me, and of course it upsets her. But she never sees Lucy. I don't think she's ever seen her. So, is there anybody?

Not really. I've been out with a few folk, of course, and since I went to London there have been a few more, mostly from dating sites, some touching serious; women in their late twenties or thirties, who have a settled life, lots of friends and a nice job and now they want a man for a long-term relationship, a short-term relationship, marriage, let's see what happens. Do you have children? No. Do you want children? Yes.

A limpid smell of rain brought Deegan to his feet. The clouds banked back in lines of grey and beyond the bog sunlight shafted through a shower.

So I take it you won't be back?

And I take it you can't leave.

Not till Mum dies. Sounds awful, I know. Do you plan to see Angela?

If I thought it was possible for her to get away and for us to meet with no one knowing, I'd be up for it. But the walls have eyes. Everyone knows or thinks they know what's going on.

I meant to say, there's a dance tonight. Angus Crawford still plays in a band – The Country Cousins – and they're on at the centre. Do you fancy going?

I'm not sure.

You'll have to make an appearance some time. They'll know you're here. And I'm on the committee, so it won't cost you.

He looked at his sister, but she never caught his eye.

Do you see much of him?

Angus?

He nodded.

Now and again. He drops round sometimes.

And he's still with Roseanne?

For the time being.

She put her head on his shoulder.

Heartbreaking, isn't it? she said.

We should be getting back. It'll rain soon.

Their mother was sleeping. The rain swept across the village for about an hour, leaving the place brighter with a single cloud in the sky, like something left over from another day.

Lorna gave her mum soup while Deegan sat on the edge of the bed and talked about London, the crowds and the noise, how he went to a concert in Hyde Park, saw a man walking down the street shouting at no one, just walking and shouting, and had been stuck in the Tube for 20 minutes. She asked if there were still speakers at Hyde Park Corner.

When she slept, Lorna phoned home and spoke to the children. She told them they would see their Uncle Andrew tomorrow. And when she had changed they sat together watching television. The dance started at eight, but there was no point in going much before nine. It finished before midnight and by that time arrangements were made for walking home or moving on to the party houses.

The village looked clean and busy. 'No Vacancies' signs marked the bed and breakfast bungalows. There was a new café, two sports equipment shops and two new hotels. The patch of green where the fairground came every summer had been landscaped into a rose garden and herbaceous border, the village hall was freshly painted white with black windows and guttering and a bright green door. The putting green was now a beer garden for one of the new hotels.

He noticed there was a new stone bridge and further up the hill a wooden bridge crossed the stretch where they jumped the burn on their way to school.

There was a smell of paint in the foyer and a notice board had replaced a photograph of the opening ceremony. Centre activities included tai chi, yoga, dance, sewing and quilting classes, a playgroup, a pensioners' lunch club and the Drop In Café was open from ten till half four every day. The Saturday Hop – Dancing to The Country Cousins – was on the last Saturday of the month from April to September.

May Wallace was at the table, issuing the tickets, and Bridie McAllister took the money. They were at the first dance he attended and he wondered why they were both needed to do a single job.

My, you're back, May Wallace said, rising from her seat to hug him when he came in. Sorry about the paint. The Ladies has just been redone, there was a bit of a problem, but it should be dry by now. You're looking well. Where are you now? Still in London? And how's your mum?

He smiled at May's multiple questions, remembering a

time when his mother told him she had met May Wallace. I think she only asked four questions, she said.

Angus was singing 'Achy Breaky Heart' and smiled when they came in. The band hadn't changed – two guitars, keyboard and drums. Angus and his cousin Matt played rhythm guitar and keyboard and sang. They worked for the electricity board. The other two came from a nearby village where the drummer Andy Simpson worked in his Dad's garage and Eddie Black worked for the council.

A mirror ball in the middle of the room and four spotlights alternating green, yellow and blue on to the dance area made it difficult to see. The tables and chairs had been pushed to the edge and, apart from three or four elderly couples, Deegan was the only man. Some girls were dancing on their own, occupying the middle of the room and swaying to the music. Cans of beer and soft drinks were served from the tea bar.

Lorna bought two cans of lager and they sat at a table near the band.

Do you think he'll be down, he said.

I'd put money on it. He'll have heard you're back. And he'll want to claim his territory.

I'm ready.

She put her hand over his.

Don't, she said. Please. Think of what it would do to Mum.

It's what it's done to me that needs to be settled. I'm not scared of him any more.

Before she could answer he walked across the floor and asked a pretty girl with too much make-up to dance. She looked sideways at her friends, smiled and followed him onto the floor.

They swayed as Angus sang 'Coat of Many Colours', sometimes glancing, finding each other, moving near, then twisting away. He noticed dust rising around the girls who were now dancing in pairs, waiting for the men to arrive. When the song finished, the girl moved away. They hadn't spoken.

Did you enjoy that? Lorna asked, as the Country Cousins

played the opening notes of 'Cripple Creek' on the keyboard to finish their first set. They replayed the notes, gradually turning up the volume till the floor was busy. Couples who'd sat for the set joined in and when the tune began everyone jumped up and down, some linking arms and swinging, others round the edge clapping in time and laughing. The set ended with a cheer.

He asked if one of them ought to run home to see if Mum was all right.

She'll be fine, said Lorna. She has her radio tuned to the World Service and spends her nights drifting in and out of sleep. She always says she never slept a wink but is sound when the carer calls in the morning.

Angus came over with four cans of lager.

The band's allowance, he said.

He sat next to Lorna and asked Deegan how long he would be around. There was an awkward silence till Angus said he would need to sort out the second set, even though everyone knew the second setlist was as predictable as the first.

The bar was busy. Bridie had moved from the reception table, but she didn't know the prices, couldn't pour pints and asked where the beers and mixers were shelved. People bought enough to see them through the second set.

Most of the younger women smoked and stood outside in the early evening chill. Someone said they thought it might rain again and there was talk of the cement factory reopening, but they weren't sure what they might be making.

It would be great for the place to get some work again, a man said.

And there was talk of another fish farm, shellfish this time.

Why wouldn't they do it, the same man said. Everything's there, all they need is the fish to stock the place.

The women in the hall refreshed their make-up and checked their phones. Some ran across the hall to show friends the latest message.

When the smokers came back the men from the pub had

arrived and the place was noisy with chatter. Then Benny Riley came in with his mates, four of them, crowding their way into the bar.

Lorna took her brother's hand. He didn't move. She turned to look at him, his face stiff and his eyes staring straight ahead, as if his body, even his heartbeat was still.

Angus crossed the hall and leaned across the table.

So we'll see you later? he said to Lorna.

She nodded.

The second set always began gently. Angus was singing 'Tennessee Waltz' and most couples stayed on the floor when they moved straight into 'Jambalaya'. The rhythm was livelier and everyone knew what to expect. There were eight songs in the second set, finishing with 'Knock Three Times' and 'Are You Lonesome Tonight?' as an encore.

Deegan stood up when the third song started.

Toilet, he said to Lorna.

I don't think you should go.

I'm fine.

Deegan was washing his hands. He heard the door open and moved towards the drier.

Benny Riley asked, You still in Edinburgh?

London.

If you're in London what're you doing here?

I'm minding my own business. What do you want, Benny?

You've got cheeky. I thought I told you not to come back.

What I do has nothing to do with you.

What you've done has to do with me though.

He knew Benny's fists were clenched and he steadied himself before moving forward. There was a touch of foam on the edge of Benny's mouth. The veins and sinews in his neck were stiff and his eyes were shiny and unfocussed. No one heard Lorna come in.

Everyone knows what happened except you, Benny, she said.

Are you here to look after your wee brother?

I'm here to see what's going on, to make sure it's a private conversation, just you and him, so nobody gets hurt. And no matter what you say, it's over. I'm going to phone Angela.

My mother's dying, Deegan said. She won't see out the summer. And I'd like her to meet her granddaughter. That's why I'm back. I came here to let my mother die with comfort and dignity.

We'll see.

That isn't an answer, Deegan said. I'm coming to the house tomorrow. I've got stuff to give my daughter and I want her to meet her granny.

He moved round Benny, left him staring, eyes like glass.

I'll be back later, Lorna said at the door. I'll see you in the morning.

The streets were wet and the air tasted of rain, the sodium strips cast an eerie light. The place was quiet, the hotels and bars were closed. In an hour there would be groups, sometimes six or eight at a time, shouting and singing, on their way to a party, or going home. And they would pair off, the way he and Angela had paired off, just to talk, to ask how things were, they had been away at university and she was sort of seeing Benny Riley, but she had been working on a film, nothing much, just as a runner, but it was great and she was sure she had made good contacts and had another interview for a job at the BBC in Glasgow and if he was still in Edinburgh, maybe they could meet up when she was down.

Everybody knew. They didn't turn up at the party and went down by the loch.

Angela told Lorna, who contacted Deegan and when he came back Benny Riley and four other forestry workers called at the house.

It's my concern now, Riley said, and we don't want to see you back here.

Angela said there were complications. The birth was

difficult. Maybe Deegan could come and see her, even if they couldn't talk. Any time he phoned, Benny Riley answered. It won't always be this way, Angela said.

He meant to take the long road home, but the rain was back, so he turned up by the school and took the trail through the woods, where Benny Riley worked.

It was a small, broadleaf wood, mostly rowan, larch and birch. The streetlights filtered long, dark shadows between occasional patches of light, sometimes reflected in the bark of the silver birches to the right of the path. And suddenly it was colder, with a strong smell of earth and damp, and a slight wind ruffled the leaves at the top of the trees.

He knew he was not alone. This was something he remembered from school. When the local boys moved through the trees and waited to ambush him, he knew they were there and turned back or climbed the hill through the woods and ran home.

Now it was too late to turn back. He did not know who was there, or how many. He stopped in the stillness and thought of climbing through the woods in the dark.

There was no moonlight and he felt his legs tremble. He moved forward slowly, and approaching the rise he could see the bridge.

Benny and his mates might not have had enough time to reach him, he thought, and they were more likely to be at the road end, on the edge of the woods across from his house because they would not know how he got home.

When he stood on the bridge he heard a rustle. The riffle of the burn obscured the noise, but something had moved, something definitely moved. He looked back the way he'd come; the path was empty and clear straight ahead.

He stared upstream, caught the traces of bluebell and red campion by the trees and the edge of primrose on the banks. Something moved to his right and moved again, but he heard no sound. He stared into the wood and when a spark of light caught its eye, he saw the hind, standing alone on the rise at the edge of the wood, still as stone and staring. He heard a rustle below and saw the movement. He stared again and heard the leaves move.

From the edge of the bank he slid down the mud to the stream, his shoes and trousers and the back of his jacket filthy, his hands cut and grazed where he tried to support himself in the fall or catch a tree.

The deer was still at the top of the hill and a fawn was lying on the bank by a pair of rowans where boys had stretched a rabbit snare. The calf was caught and the more it tugged the tighter the trap became. It looked at him trembling, its sides caving in and out and he caught the sudden smell of fear.

He tried to climb the bank and slipped, tried again and caught his foot on a rock, using the hold to approach the fawn. As he moved forward he heard the moan and the scrape as it tried to leave, pulling at the snare.

Suddenly, Deegan thought of the hind. It was close and he caught the hot, sharp stink.

It's okay, he said. Shush now, quiet, easy now, easy.

He looked up at the deer and positioned himself side on and above the calf, kneeling in the mud. When he touched the trapped forepaw, the calf started kicking and the leg slipped through his fingers. He caught it and again it slipped. He grabbed and held and when he touched the wire, the fawn stopped kicking.

He could see the gleam of blood and the leg was wet from where the doe had nuzzled the wound. The snare was tight and the wire stiff, there was a slight swelling around the wound but he tugged on the noose and suddenly it moved. He straightened the wire, gradually slipping the noose till there was enough space to lift the leg free.

He looked up in time to see the hind turn and watched the fawn slip up the bank.

Someone always robs the poor

My father said, We're next.

He said it as Dora's cart disappeared through the mud with me waving. And he said it working in the field. I could hear him as I cut the corn, bound and stacked the sheaves. I looked up and he was smiling: We're next, he said.

And thirty-four days later he caught me reading *The Wonders of Science*, a book Dora had left. He fed it to the pig he'd sold to a man on the other side of the village, an old man who asked girls for a kiss. He told me, I have your pig, and your father comes here to feed words to the pig. Do you think it will talk to me?

I was watching the pig eat my book of fairy stories when my father grabbed my arm. Miriam, he said. Come on. We're next.

We packed what we had and I had nothing. Two dresses, a pair of shoes, two pairs of stockings, underwear, a scarf and a blanket were crammed into a sack my mother stole from the miller, in with my mother's clothes and my sister's clothes. My sister Christina and I sat on the board at the end of the cart, my mother sat on a bale of straw, clutching the miller's sack, and my father stood behind us at the back of the cart, waving his hat till we passed two fields and turned a corner on the road to Warsaw.

All day my father stood at the back of the cart waving his hat, and when my mother told him to sit down, he said, I am waving goodbye to Poland. I am looking to see what I have to take with me.

We reached Warsaw at night. The cart stopped in a square. Father paid the driver and he left without a word. We were at the door of a ticket agent's office and just before we settled down to sleep, my mother produced black bread from the sack and tore a piece for everyone. Then she went to the wall with a can and water came out.

Christina cried because she thought the devil was in the wall. Water came from the well but now it was coming from the *mur*. I slept with my mother's arm around me and Christina's head on my lap.

We were wakened in the morning by a peddler who took the can to a house and came back with hot water, which we drank with the bread. By the time the agent arrived to open the shop there were seven or eight other families on the doorstep. The agent kept us waiting till a girl in a red dress arrived. Then the man let us into the shop one family at a time, standing by the door and directing us to the counter where the girl asked for our passports, returning them with tickets she said would take us to New York.

We followed the crowd to the railway station. My father showed everyone his ticket, asking where he got the train to America.

A man with gold braid on his shoulder and a book on a string hanging from his belt put us on a train. We waited in the station for fourteen hours, going to the toilet with Christina and my mother twice while my father talked to the other men with tickets, some for New York, some for Boston, but mostly for Chicago.

One man said he would open a tailor shop; another would have a bakery, with fresh bread rolls and butter running down the side every morning. They smiled when my father said he would plant crops and harvest them.

We were sleeping when the train jolted us forward. There was a clank and a tug. Christina fell off the bench and cried; I watched the yellow lights pass through the dirty glass and Father stood by the window waving his hat.

We travelled slowly. People sold food and drinks on station platforms. I tasted coffee and loved it from the first sip.

A man with a small green accordion kept us merry playing happy tunes and songs we knew or could easily learn. Everyone was singing and clapping hands, making music any way they could. Then we shook hands and wished each other good night and a safe journey. I remember thinking it was silly, shaking hands when we were all on the same train.

This was how we travelled for two nights.

It was dark when the border guards came with lanterns that turned faces the colour of corn. I do not remember feeling the train stop. The sway of the carriage and the wheels ticking like a clock sent me to sleep, even though the slatted benches were solid and I wakened stiff and stood trying to stretch myself in the place that smelled of bodies.

A tall thin man in uniform told me to sit on my mother's knee. He looked at our passports and tickets and told us to leave the train, told us we could not travel through Germany.

One of the men in the compartment, a young man with beautiful eyes and dark curly hair, but a flat and twisted, ugly mouth, put his hand on my father's arm as he was about to speak. The young man took the guard to one side and they talked. Then he spoke to my father. I don't know what he said, but my father told him, I have a ticket for America.

The young man smiled and nodded as he whispered, explaining what would become obvious, that my father would need to give the guard some money or we would be thrown off the train. Then I moved closer and heard the young man's voice harden as he explained an extra payment was necessary, over and above the price of his ticket, money for the guard, which my father understood. He said this was what he was leaving behind in Poland.

The young man explained again.

No, my father said.

Eventually, the young man grew exasperated and asked if

my father had money. Yes, he said, producing bills from inside his coat. The young man took one and gave it to the guard and the guard walked away.

Thief, my father shouted at the young man.

He kept it up throughout the night. My mother was grim. She drew us into her, covering us with her coat as she whispered, almost spitting the words towards my father, telling him to be quiet, that he was shaming us and to let us rest.

Next morning when the train stopped to take on water, my father, who had not slept all night, started shouting at the young man he said had stolen his money. The young man approached my father and put a bank note into his hand. He took my father's bag and my mother's sack and threw them off the train. When my father jumped down onto the tracks to collect the luggage, the young man lifted me and Christina down from the wagon. I can remember the cold on my legs, the throb of fear. My mother followed us, jumping from the van to see if we were safe while my father gathered the bags and scattered clothes. And the young man closed the wagon door.

My father ran up and down the tracks shouting, pleading and shaking his fist till the train left us stranded.

My mother and father started arguing.

You should have given him the money, she said.

What for? My father said. We have tickets.

And what good are they now?

The station was empty. No one: maybe birds singing and people working in the fields, maybe a horse and cart or a woman walking through the village, but not much else. We stayed at a place we never knew, for two nights, till we had no more food. On the third day while my father was sleeping my mother went into the village and came back with bread and milk and jam.

Two days later, when the food ran out, my father told my mother to get more food, asking if she could find some ham and cheese.

Take the child, he said. Take Miriam.

She took my hand and led me down the hill and into the village to a small shop with a house at the back. She walked into the shop where a man was working at a table. He looked up and smiled.

My mother told me to sit by the door and to say nothing, to stay still, even if someone came to the door. The man pulled the blind down to the bottom of the window and locked the door. My mother went with him into the back of the shop.

I knew it wasn't right. It was something I could not understand, even though I knew it was simple. It was like finding a big word. I knew if I remembered everything, the dark room turned green by the blind, the way light caught the edge of the counter, the yellow cheeses and pink ham, the jars and their labels, especially the way I felt waiting on my mother, I would understand it some time soon.

My mother at that time was a young woman, maybe twenty-four or twenty-five. My father was more than forty. I have a photograph of my mother taken when she was eighteen and she was very beautiful. So it was easy for her, she could get us whatever was needed. I knew that then. I understood that life is easier if you are beautiful, though other people envy you. But I now know my mother didn't feel beautiful.

When she came out of the shop, the man turned the key in the lock, pulled up the blind and smiled at me. My mother had a basket of food. She turned her back to the man and put money into her underwear. And when we were on the street she knelt down and faced me.

Not a word, she said. Do not tell anyone what happened or what you saw.

My mother got us to Hamburg.

My father said we would get a train because we had a ticket.

My mother spoke to the stationmaster who spoke to the guard and a train took us to another station.

See, my father said, all is well. They are letting us on the train because we have a ticket. And we have paid for the ticket and do not have to pay any more, not to robbers or cheats, thieves or anyone.

He said the German people were very generous, giving us such fine food and helping us. If anyone asked, he said we were robbed, then tricked, and a man the devil had cursed with a twisted mouth threw us off the train.

It was raining when we arrived in Hamburg early next morning. My father stood still in the middle of the station while people swirled around us. We huddled together, the four of us; my father muttered prayers because he did not know where to go. A policeman approached and my father told him we had tickets for America. The policeman shook his head and looked at my mother who looked at the ground. My father showed him the tickets.

The policeman led us out of the station and pointed down a road and we walked for hours in the mud and rain, till we came to the river where there were tall cranes and barges.

My father showed the tickets and people shook their heads.

America, he said.

Eventually, the police took us to a big shed with hundreds of men sitting on crates and cases, smoking and nodding when someone spoke. Some were playing cards and there were groups watching, maybe waiting for someone to drop out.

The women were gathered in a corner, sitting on blankets, playing with the children, cooking. There was a smell of warmth and sweat. Some women were crying.

My mother looked around us, leaned back and closed her eyes, with her head against the wall. Someone always robs the poor, she said.

There were more languages than I had ever heard, in fact that was when I learned there were more than one or two languages in the world, some sounded similar, but the differences became obvious when the women spoke or children screamed instructions, running round full of life in a place that looked and smelled like purgatory.

America, my father said.

And a man with a grey beard nodded.

I will check the tickets, my mother said, to see if we are in the right place.

No, my father said, I will check the tickets.

You speak to that man and find out when the boat leaves and where it goes to in America, she said. I will find the ticket office.

I thought she was gone a long time. And just when I was trying not to think of the green blind and the noise of dying breath, she appeared and told my father the ticket office was shut, then she pulled her shawl around her and went to sleep.

We were wakened by a whistle. Everyone stood up and started shuffling, to keep warm at first, then moving towards the doors at the far end of the shed.

This way, my mother said. Our tickets go this way.

All day we waited with nothing to eat or drink. My father smoked and stared ahead, occasionally wondering when they would take his ticket and let him board the ship. My mother told him to be patient.

Why do we have to wait here? he asked. No one else is waiting here.

Because I could not show our tickets to the official. You would not let me handle the tickets, so he told us to wait here and he will come for us.

We could see the ship, grey and red with black smoke bursting from the funnels and people trying to run up the gangplanks. Some were sick and had to be carried, one man crawled part of the way on his hands and knees till two others helped him. Eventually there was no one boarding and my father became very agitated.

My mother told us to wait. She would go and see the official. My father paced the platform until my mother appeared with two men. One of the men motioned us towards the end of the building where my mother was waiting with the other man. Give me the tickets, she said to my father.

I will present the tickets, he said as a policeman arrived with a dog at the end of a chain. They shouted in German and the man who had taken our tickets replied.

Looking back, I believe we were told to stay for the policeman turned back the way he came, shouting and running towards a hut.

Come on, said the man. Quickly.

In the cool afternoon air, we ran as though it was raining across wet wood and cobbles, slipping and constantly fearful of the barking dogs behind us. My father carried his case and my mother's sack and she carried Christina. I ran holding on to her skirts and slipped many times on the wood at the front of the harbour.

The man hurried us along to the front of the ship, where we went down a ramp and walked along a ledge below the harbour into the boat where wood was stacked. It was dark, but we could smell the wood. There was also a smell of oil and burning fat.

We were taken through what must have been the belly of the boat and left in a corner, behind some crates, and told to be still. My mother told us to be quiet, told us we were not to move from this place, that we would be moved in with the others when the boat sailed.

I thought the ticket office was shut, my father said.

And she looked at him.

If the ticket office was shut, how did you know these men who brought us here?

And at this the whistle went shuddering through the boat. There was shouting and a great clanking of chains, ropes hitting the side and we were all very scared, especially when the engine started and we felt the pull of the boat and knew this noise would be with us till we reached America.

I have told you, my mother shouted, the ticket office was

shut for me because you had the tickets, because you did not trust your wife to show the man the tickets you had bought with money she had earned as well as you. I asked these men and told them my husband had the tickets and if the police, who were looking for escaped refugees, had not arrived he would have taken your tickets. But tell me now, what difference does it make? Are we on the boat? Are we going away? Have we set sail? Are we, at last, going to America?

It was dark when they wakened Christina and me, telling us to be quiet. We were led along corridors and up stairways to the main hold of the ship. There were no hammocks and we spent the journey lying on the floor, everyone feeling ill and wailing, people being sick around us.

We were two nights at sea and landed one morning.

America, my father shouted, and people strained to see above the sea at the portholes.

A man shouted something and my father gathered us together and took us onto the deck where we waited with maybe 40 or 50 other people. When the gangplank was secured we landed.

We stood on the quayside while some crates were unloaded. This is America, my father said. He walked through the gates and no one stopped him.

Now we must find a place to stay, he said.

When he stopped people in the street they hurried on. He went into a shop to buy milk and handed the money he brought from Poland.

They are refusing my money, he said.

Have you heard of the dollar? my mother asked and he looked at her, trying to understand.

Where can I get dollars? he said.

She suggested they go to a bank.

We walked up a big wide street, peering into shops to see if they were banks. People looked at us strangely. I hid in my mother's skirts, but my father took no notice. We obviously looked strange, were darker skinned, had strange clothes and we must have smelled. We hadn't washed and had been in the hold of a boat that stank.

We stopped at a corner, my father wondering which way to turn, when a young man in a suit approached us.

Excuse me, he said. Are you Polish?

Jan took us to his mother's house where we ate, bathed in front of a big fire and slept in a bed, all four of us together.

In the morning my father was full of questions. Where could we find a place to stay? Where could he find work? And where could he change his money into dollars?

That was when we discovered we had landed at Leith and were now in Edinburgh. My father thought because the boat had landed we were in America. Jan told us the police were very strict on people getting into the country, that no matter how we had arrived, we would need to be very careful. He would take us to Glasgow where we could get a boat for America.

I have a ticket, my father said.

Jan looked at my father's ticket and threw it into the fire. It's worthless, he told him.

My father stared at the fire, tears breaking on the edge of his eyes. Jan explained the ticket would only take us from Warsaw to Germany.

But I had a ticket to America, my father said. That was my ticket to America.

And when Jan was explaining how he would have needed to show his passport to get a ticket for America, he asked: Then why am I here?

Jan explained again. And my father looked at my mother with wonder in his eyes: Why are we here? he asked. How did we get here from where we were? How did we get on the boat without showing our passports and no one asked for our tickets? Is that why we are here instead of America?

The boat was going to America, but we got off too soon because you thought this was America, my mother said.

Everyone I spoke to asked where my ticket was and I told them, My husband has the tickets, and they believed me. That's how we got here. Good fortune.

I could see by the way Jan looked at my mother that he did not believe her. He turned his head, blushed slightly and left the room; and when he came back he stared at her as though he could see through her, stared and would not stop. Every time I looked up he was staring at my mother and I think that was why we came to Glasgow, to work and save and buy tickets for America because the boats for America left from here.

The reason they are being strict about immigrants and the reason why you will find it difficult to get a job here or in America is because of the banks, Jan told us. And my father nodded in agreement.

Only the main branches are open, Jan said. The other smaller branches open only at certain times.

I don't want a job in a bank, my father said. And my mother left the room.

I think the American banks will be opened, my father said. If they have been closed for some time they will not have any money because people will not have been able to put money into the banks because they are closed, so they will need to open to take people's money, so I think we will go to America.

That night when Jan came home from work, he spoke privately with his mother then sat us round the table and said it had been arranged. He would take us to Glasgow.

We left next morning and by nightfall we had pound notes, ten shilling notes, silver and copper coins. We had rented a single room in Tradeston, on the south side of the river, with a toilet on the landing we shared with three other families, one from Germany, one from Ireland and the others in the building were Russian.

Jan gave my mother some money, I think it was thirty shillings, and took her to the dairy by the next close. My mother told us he had left three pounds with the man, who was Polish.

That night we sat in the filthy room lit by a single gas lamp and heated by a black kitchen range that glowed red and leaked smoke from the cracks.

We sat on the floor, ate meat and potatoes and drank milk. My father looked out the window. We sat with my mother who told us the story of the old man and the boy who could not catch fish. Then for the first time since we left Poland we stripped ourselves naked and stood by the sink while kettles boiled and the windows steamed and my mother washed us all over and we knelt on the sticky floor and dried our hair in front of the fire. My father asked my mother where the dock was and what was the name of the man Jan had told him to see.

Two days later he was working. He and the other men had to pass through lines of men who spat on you when you went to work. This work lasted two days, but he must have been a good worker for they told him to come back the following week; and that's how it went, my father working perhaps two or three days a week, my mother scrubbing the house till, by the end of the week, there was a smell of carbolic and disinfectant and we could see the pattern on the linoleum and the morning light came through the window.

She helped the Irish women pick rags or she would help the Russians with their sewing and from this she would bring home scraps of material and make curtains for the window and sew rags together to make a rug for the front of the fire.

The Irish boy next door took Christina and I to school. The women told my mother. I don't know how they understood each other, but one morning instead of going to sit on the stair or hang on to my mother all day, she washed us and when we had hot milk and bread and jam she knocked on the next door's door and smiled at the woman and pushed us towards her. Go, she said to us. Go and get a better life.

Christina thought she was leaving and never coming back. She knew we weren't in America and perhaps she thought that was where we were being sent, but my mother told her where we were going and why, though she didn't want to go with the Irish boy who never spoke but left us standing in front of a teacher and ran away.

That's when my name changed. Miss Ritchie called me Mirren and that was my name all through school. We had never been to school and we did not know our birthday and we knew nothing about papers, so they sent an older girl who came from Warsaw to see my mother who asked my father to go to the school and he said school was wasted on girls, so my mother went. I do not know how we were registered, but it happened.

We started in the infant class, but after a few months we progressed. Miss Ritchie gave us extra lessons, always in writing and reading and arithmetic and every night my mother sat us down at the table and took us through our lessons.

Years later I realised we could have told her anything, could have said we had done our homework and left the pages blank because my mother could neither read nor write, but she sat with us, watching us, smiling. My father complained about the cost of the extra heating and lighting, and kept on about being cheated.

Then one night everything changed. He was staring into the fire and my mother was washing Christina at the sink. I was copying letters and numbers into my jotter.

Stand up, my father said.

My mother must have ignored him for he shouted it, telling her to turn round and face him.

He came across and put his hands on her stomach. What's this? he said.

She went white. I saw the colour leave her face immediately. There was a piece of metal we used as a poker. My father picked it up and slashed my mother across the face. The blood gushed from her cheek and ran through her fingers. He hit her across the head and when she heard the crack Christina screamed and ran to me and we watched as my mother lay on the floor and my father exhausted himself hitting her with the poker. Then he turned on himself, banging his head against the wall till blood ran all the way to the floor.

My mother hauled herself onto the chair, and when he finished and his face was red in the gaslight and she was shaking, holding herself tightly, she started speaking and he listened, shaking his head through his sobs.

My mother held a cold, wet cloth to her face. My father stood by the wall, sobbing as she spoke, cuddling himself, rocking back and forward on his heels.

Why do you think I married you? she said. For shame, because you came to my house and told my father you would give him a horse and I had nowhere else to go and you didn't even know about me and Peter. We'd run and meet and hide and you never knew. You thought I was working. Everyone knew, but you didn't know. Even when Peter's children were born, you didn't know.

And when you said you would take us to America, what could I do but go. And I would have been a good wife, but you were too stupid to have a good wife, too mean and too proud to ask, thinking you knew everything while people robbed you and laughed because you are a poor and stupid, ignorant peasant who thinks he knows everything and knows nothing and is easy to cheat.

Now he was listening. His mouth was open and he looked at her as though for the first time.

I know why you wanted to go to America. Your mother knew about Peter and me. How could you not know? You must have been told. She would have told you, but you would not believe her because you are too proud. But you could not ignore what your mother tells you, so you decided to end your shame and take us to America.

But you buy a ticket without knowing the price and get thrown off the train when it reaches Germany because that's as far as your ticket goes and you go on believing the lie and are so mean you will not even give the guard enough to take you through Germany. You could have sat on that train to Hamburg for the price of a slice of ham, but you left us stranded.

How do you think we got food? The Germans are kind, you said. To Poles? How do you think we got a lift to Warsaw for what you paid the driver? How do you think we got on the train and then on the boat and how do you think we survived? Do you mean to say you lay in that hold among those boxes and didn't even wonder what we were doing there when everyone else was in another part of the boat? And why are we here instead of America?

I don't know whose baby you've killed, but you can rest knowing it isn't your baby. Now let's see how you survive. I have fed my children and seen to them. You think they are yours. I know they are mine.

He was gone by morning and I never saw my father for more than 20 years. When we asked where he was, my mother would laugh and say, America.

We had a strange life in that room. We were always poor, or on the edge of poverty. My mother worked and I left school at 14 and worked. Christina was our hope. But of all the terrible times, nothing was worse than when Christina died.

She was 13 when she was kicked by a horse. I came home from my work as a sewing machinist and a neighbour told me she was in hospital. She slipped, fell in front of the horse and was never the same. She lost everything gradually. No matter what we did. One morning she couldn't speak, then she couldn't hear and so it went until she was an invalid and we had to change her twice or three times a day. She died one morning after breakfast. I fed her and had gone to wash my hands. When I turned round she was looking at me in a way I had never seen before, she was pleading. I was afraid and called for my mother and we sat with Christina for two hours watching life leave her.

She was buried two days later. That was the last time I saw my father. He was at the cemetery, waiting for the hearse to arrive. And he stood at the grave and left on his own. He did not speak.

After a time, we left the Tradeston room and came here to this house. My mother died here and every day I think of her. She wanted my life to be different, better than her life. In some ways it has been better. But she was lonely, here in a strange place. Not that she wanted me to stay. Go out, she told me. Meet a young man. Be happy. But it never happened. When I was younger I would liked to have married, then I saw what married life was like and decided things were better as they were.

She worked, my mother, first in a dairy, then in a butcher's shop till she went cleaning for the butcher, Mr Gilchrist. He and his wife were very good to us. Mrs Gilchrist recommended my mother to her friends and Mr Gilchrist always made sure we had meat on the table.

Of course, I wondered. My mother said, We are leaving Tradeston, and that was all. I never asked, about anything, where her presents came from. Nothing grand, a ring or two, brooches, necklaces, small personal gifts, some of them would have cost a pretty penny, but she never spoke.

She gave up cleaning when her clients died. One time there were five and within 18 months, two years at most, there were none. She went to classes, learned to read and write and spell and then stayed at home, drank tea, listened to the wireless, went to the library and read a book a week, stories about Poland mostly, always talking about the place she called home, wondering if Marietta was married, if Agata had children, if Jacob still wore the straw hat with flowers, if Dorota went to Warsaw, if Anna's mother went blind, if Augustyn ever sold his horse, if Peter was alive and if he was dead, could she visit his grave. She wanted to go back, but we never went and now I've been here seventy years, an illegal immigrant.

Queen's Park

Spring

Andrew John Murphy, 67, retired:
It's only since the wife died.

And all I do is look. I sit on a bench and watch them, chattering past.

They remind me of the flamingoes we saw in the Camargue.

Sheila wanted to see the white horses. She imagined them running along the beach, but it was the end of October and the flamingoes were white. I thought they would still be pink, but they change colour in winter. And the horses stood at the roadside, waiting to be fed.

I was on a platform and all you could see was flatland, marshes that stretched for miles. And two flamingoes came in to land. They spread their wings and hopped along the ground, settling in the slurry water, then standing tall and straight on one leg.

That's why they remind me of flamingoes. Their legs; awkward, long and slender. Just to see them. Beautiful.

I've never spoken and I'm sure they don't even know I exist. They never look at me, but pass in bunches, huddled together, absorbed, as if I'm not there.

I never smile or try to interrupt their conversation because I don't want them to think I'm a creepy old man. But one of them must be lonely. She might be shy and maybe even wants to talk, but wouldn't know how, so I have thought about some questions to ask. Who's her favourite teacher? What's her favourite TV show, her favourite music, favourite food, does she like pizzas, ice cream, that sort of thing? I'd save fashion till last and tell her she'd look great in that, lovely.

I watch and sometimes think I see her at the end of a group. She isn't the popular one, the pretty one, the one everybody wants to be with; no one would notice if she wasn't there, but she wants to belong and tags along, hoping to be recognised.

Andrea Rose Byrne, 24, Teacher:
St Brendan's Primary School
Primary 4 Springtime Ramble
Topic – Biology (Gathering Frog Spawn)
Present – Josie, Abel, Kimberley, Tommy, Ali, Jena, Sam, Afina, Rodika, Tania, Habib, Rachel, James, Andrew, Bassam, Nelu, Jacob, Harry, Bruno, Sorcha, Heather, Billy, Angus, Flora, Sarah, Marjorie, Rhona, Ana, Irene, Bronagh.
Report – No child brought spare clothes or wellingtons. We took 10 photographs and gathered two jars of frogspawn. Andrew, Rodika and Sarah became anxious when their trainers got dirty. Jacob pushed Rachel. She fell but was uninjured. Billy said he saw an eagle.

Amber Connor, 19, mother:
That bit at my side's still sore. I caught the corner of the table when I fell; it made me scream and wakened the baby.
Look what you've done, he said. You've wakened the fucken wean. Jesus Christ. Can you no do anything right.
It was black and blue this morning. And the other lump hasn't healed. It's taking a long time to go. I thought it would be down by now, but it's still the same.
I told the doctor I fell.
You can tell me, he said.
I'm telling you. I fell.
You don't get something like this from falling.
So if he knows and the nurse knows and my Mum knows, who else knows? Who else did I waken? The guy downstairs told me, If you want any help let me know.
But the wean needs to see his Daddy.

I know what'll happen. It'll be the same as before. He'll be sorry and promise, swear on the wean's life it'll never, never ever happen again.

That's it, he said last time. And he was okay, not off it, never actually off it, but he seemed to be handling it for a week or two.

But he'll be back on it today because he still has money. So I need to stay out. He'll waken at the back of two, go down to the pub and won't be back till after 11 and I should be sleeping by then, but I was sleeping last night when he came in and wakened me because he'd had nothing to eat.

If I leave something out for him, sandwiches, he can have them when he comes in. As long as he doesn't try to make chips. He nearly set the place on fire when he fell asleep watching telly with the chip pan on. Thank God I wakened.

I'll need to stay out till three, maybe four o'clock to be on the safe side. I'll get a pot noodle for the wean.

And hope it stays dry.

Summer

William Robert Smith, 29, Unemployed:
The old guy had one of these slinger things; it makes the ball go further. He had this slinger and a tennis ball; nice dog though, Border Collie, lovely, clever dogs them. They know what it's about, Border Collies. They're sheep dogs.

The guy slings the ball and the dog gets it, then Mo and Chaz charge after it, his dog drops the ball and Geezer picks it up.

Took ages, ten minutes, more, nearly half an hour to get Geezer to drop the ball. He was a police dog and was trained to hold on to things. And this guy's waiting, all the time, just standing there. I told him he'd get his ball back, cause if Geezer gets a ball, the other two'll want one and I'll have to get a slinger thing to throw the ball and that's just daft.

He got his ball back. I just threw it at him: There's your ball,

I said, even though it was the dog's ball.

But it was his dog that dropped it. Geezer just lifted the ball another dog dropped.

Amrita Kaur, 27, Lawyer:
I don't know. I haven't seen her for a while. But she'll be back. She comes and goes; wears the same brown woollen coat summer or winter with the same low-at-the-ankle fur-lined boots. Every day she moves between families, gathering their rubbish and when her arms are full, she takes it to the bin. When the bin's full, she piles the litter at the side, newspapers folded and laid together, sandwich wrappers and tissues in a tied plastic bag, cans flattened and piled across each other.

Cherie Ann Ross, 17, Unemployed:
You've to be out by half nine and you can't get in till after seven. And you've to have finished breakfast – tea, roll and spread – and your bed's to be made by the time you leave.

Me and Shell used to sit in the bus shelter and blether, but she got moved. She'd send us texts and that, but she doesn't send them now. Her phone must be out of credit.

My phone's been out of juice sometimes. I used to buy a phone card when I got my money. I'd buy them from the old Paki guy, but he started getting creepy, saying things like, Hello Sexy when I came into his shop and did I want a card for nothing so I have to buy a dearer card from that other guy, him by the bus stop. It's the only thing I go in for, so he's okay. Sometimes it's his wife and she looks at you as if you had some kind of disease you'd pass on just coming into the place; takes your money, but.

The park's great. Most of the time nobody bothers you. Most women don't stay. They pass through, on their way to some place else. And there's usually guys sleeping on the benches, mornings anyway. They're up the hill, by the bit where the lassie was murdered, where they've put up a wee sign with her name.

I go up there. Then I climb the steps, go up to the flagpole and sit for a while, come down and go back three or four times. That way nobody bothers you.

I love to go there, love to go up and see the sun on the hills, especially when a cloud crosses it. It's at the other end of the city, further than that, dead far away. I don't know where they are, but I'd love to go there, love to see them up close, climb that wee hill at the end and see if I could see back to here, look at the flagpole and say, I've been there.

Sometimes I get lost in a wee dream, just sitting there, trying to count the spires, or there's a nice glint on the roofs after it's been raining and there's the shiny, new buildings. I look at the birds, the way they take off and twist in the air. I don't understand why pigeons take off from the grass and settle on the roof, then take off from the roof, fly away then land back on the roof. It must be that they get fed up in the one place, doing the same thing and even though they end up in the same place, at least they've done something in between, something that makes it less boring.

Still, I'm better off than some folk. You see them here, guys in wheelchairs that need carers. I think I'd be good at it. Looking after folk.

Autumn

Agnes Mary Walker, 84, Retired:
I used to bring the children here, Primaries Three and Four, usually at the start of the class year when the park walkways and verges are covered with leaves. The children collected leaves, pasted them into their jotters and wrote a little sentence or two about autumn and their day out, what they did and how they enjoyed it.

Of course, I always told them the park's history, about Mary, Queen of Scots and the Battle of Langside, about the Camphill Mansion and how I used to come here when I was little. And I asked them to imagine what it was like during the war when there were allotments growing soft fruit and vegetables.

We'd come here after church. Mummy would run home to put on the potatoes and veg, reheat the meat and do the gravy for Sunday dinner. This wasn't during The War, of course. There was scarcely any meat then.

The week's smoke had disappeared and Sundays were always clear. You could see across the city to the Campsies. I know you can do that now, but it wasn't like that then. Seeing across the city was one of the things that made Sundays special.

Daddy, my little sister Molly and I used to climb the hill. We would run up here, play hide-and-seek in the bushes and skip back down the hill. Daddy never climbed the hill. He used to shout on us to be careful and stood by the bandstand smoking his pipe.

I'd like to get back up there and see the view again. I haven't been up to the flagpole in years, but I well remember the slippery steps and imagine they are still slippery.

Poor Molly. I often wonder what her daughter would have been like, what kind of auntie I'd have been. I'd like to think she could have spoken to me about the things girls can't always tell their mothers, or even their friends sometimes. I'd have enjoyed taking her places, showing her my favourite things, trips to the Art Galleries and Saturday concerts.

I think of her when I see these girls in the park now. Many are foreign, of course, but I'm sorry to say, our girls don't show them any kind of example.

And it isn't just in the way they dress, though that's bad enough, it's the language they use. And not just the swearing, it's the harshness of it. And the girls are worse than the boys. You do expect that sort of thing from boys, showing off and swearing, but not from girls. It's as if they're trying to beat the boys at their own game, smoking in the street and using foul language.

Of course, it's normal nowadays. I was speaking to Mrs Alexander who had her handbag stolen, and I asked which one. The nigger brown one, she said.

And we laughed.

So I've lived long enough to hear my mother's favourite colour become a swear word and for the f-word to be printed in newspapers and heard on the BBC.

But so much has changed. There's a sign by the duck pond telling people not to feed the ducks because it attracts vermin. I suppose they mean rats; but children love to feed the ducks and to deny them that pleasure because rats might eat the bread is surely taking things too far, especially when there are so many more important issues to deal with.

Feeding the ducks is one of the joys of winter. Of course, the weather's so awful I don't always go now, though I do like to see the leaves swirl and watch the children jump to catch them. It makes me think of spring and look forward to the fresh shoots and lighter nights.

David McKay, 47, Unemployed:
She varnished my hair to the headboard. So I paid Wee Carrie to cut my hair off the fucken board, couldnae move, man. You want to've seen the state of my heid. Had to borrow the money back off her but.

Then I had this great idea. I was skint, and the wife had two pair of glasses, so I tried to sell one of the pairs. I mean, Jesus Christ, you can only wear one pair at a time. Tried to pawn them. Got fuck all. The guy never said nothing. Just looked at us and pulled the shutter down.

Then maybe two or three days later, she said she was going to get the milk. And a week later I got a postcard from London. It said, *Cheerio.*

That's the two of them away now. I'm on my Jack Jones. But she'll be back.

I just come up here to pass the time. There's eight of us, regulars, the Garden Party. We meet up the back of the greenhouses. Whoever gets his money that day brings up the drink, with two saving up for the weekend and one with a day to spare. It's communism, man, fucken telling you, pure communism. One for all, know what I mean.

I just come up here till she gets back, and she'll definitely be back. She's hopeless on her own, hopeless.

Peter Devlin, 36, Lorry Driver:
Thursday nights.

It's the only time I can make it.

Thing is, I used to work late on a Thursday, get home after 10 and go straight to bed, but when the cutbacks started and the overtime stopped, I never told her, so I get a curry after work and have an hour or two in Bissell's, where I've met one or two guys before now.

I need a couple of whiskies, need to feel braver. You can call it Dutch courage if you like, but it works for me.

And I always take the long way, stay to the path at the edge of the park before going in towards the bushes and the gardens. And I take a half bottle, just in case I get nervous, and have a slug or two before moving in to the centre.

Last time there were a couple of guys on the pathway, with two others watching, so I stood around and offered a young lad a slug of whisky. And it was great, the first time I actually wanted to see someone afterwards.

A few weeks ago the wife asked if the cutbacks were affecting me. I said they'd started and there was likely to be more, so there were regular union meetings on a Thursday, but apart from that things were carrying on much as before.

When I get home, the kids are in bed and the wife's in the bath.

How was your meeting? she asks.

Winter

Mohammad Alim Khan, 28, Waiter:
In summer, there's a guy who sometimes prays at the top of the

park. I found him by accident. He lays out his mat, kneels down and prays. It felt like an intrusion, as if I shouldn't be there, seeing him like that.

I was looking for squirrels. The ones along the pathway get plenty, but there must be others who get nothing, so I went up to see if I could find them.

I turned back when I saw him, but he won't be up there now, praying in this weather, so I'll maybe take a run up and see if I can see them.

It's important to feed them in winter, especially when there's snow on the ground. I bring a bag of peanuts in by the side gate, missing the busiest parts, the rose garden and boating pond in summer, the hot house in winter, stand in front of the railings and wait. They come out slowly, but there's always one that's brave or hungry enough to lead the others. When it reaches the last nut it sometimes waits for me to put another nut down.

They can feed from my hand and in summer, late spring and early autumn they climb onto my arm, but when it's raining or windy, in the cold weather they don't seem to expect me, and sometimes take a long time to come.

And just as quick, they leave me standing and I have to move on. I watch them when they cross the path and scramble up a tree. I love the way their tails wave when they run.

Margaret Donaghy, 56, Social Worker:
There's this big guy and every time he passes the woman with the headscarf selling *The Big Issue* by the park gates, he says, Fuck off, useless cunt. Fuck off back to where you came from.

And she smiles because he speaks to her.

Michael James Anderson, 73, Retired:
Glasgow becomes quieter when you reach a certain age.

These mornings a mist hangs over the park, leaves stick to the pavements and breath stains the air.

I get up at six and watch the sun rise. It's funny the way the city comes together; more people, more noise and the rising sun.

I never used to come here, passed it every day, at least twice a day and didn't bother, never even looked. But when I retired I thought I need to keep myself active, so I started coming into the park, just for a walk in the afternoons when Margaret was sleeping.

Then I'd bring her. When she could climb up to the glasshouse it was lovely, something new for her every day. By that time she couldn't remember being here the day before and sat as contented as you like watching the goldfish, or looking at the birds in their cages. She hardly ever spoke, but I knew she was happy just sitting there.

The place has a lot of young mothers and children, and while I wouldn't grudge them their activities, they are a bit noisy. Margaret watched the fish and I read the paper, always keeping an eye on her. She stood in the passageway and stared at the water. People just moved round her.

Then, when she couldn't manage the hill, we sat on a bench and she seemed very contented, though it was always difficult. One never knew how things would turn out. I suppose it was the progression of her illness, but there was no way of knowing that then, the sudden mood swings, the way she would shout at me to leave her alone. I'll tell my mother on you, she'd say, and walk away. When I caught up with her five minutes later, she was fine, would come home, eat her tea and watch television till she was nearly sleeping and I'd get her ready for bed.

She'd sleep all day now, if I let her, but I try to keep her awake, keep her active. They're going to have another assessment soon and there's talk of her going into care. I don't suppose it'll make much difference to her, but I'll miss her, miss the routine.

And if she's not here, I'll be on a single person's pension. Things are hard enough as it is, but without the extra we get for the two of us, I don't know what I'll do. I'll need to get a job, something part-time, I suppose.

So it's a lot to think about. It's a worry. Which is why I like to get up early, wash and shave, have some tea and a slice of toast, then come over here while it's dark and there's a lovely chill in the air. And sit, sit here when it's quiet, sit till the sun comes up, then go home, see to Margaret and start our day.

After the dance

It was afterwards, when everyone was hanging around, she noticed Jamsie Fallon. He was on his own, away from the crowd. She remembered feeling sorry for him, the lost way he had about him, as if he knew there was something missing, but didn't know what it was or how to find it. That sort of thing was always more noticeable in big men, their bits of awkwardness and difficulties seemed to stand out more.

She never thought. He didn't live up her way, but he tagged on with Fraser while she and Annie walked together as far as McArthur's Field. When Fraser stopped to light a smoke, Annie held her coat open against the breeze, though there was hardly any wind, and they sort of paired off, walking in front and bumping into each other, nudging, the way you do to get the thrill of a touch, or so she imagined for she had never wanted that or even thought about it. But afterwards it was the most obvious thing.

Nice night, he said.

She asked where he was going and he said he was just seeing Fraser back, for it was a long road to be walking on your own. And it was a grand night with a good full moon and he liked that, liked watching the shadows and the changes in the land, the way trees looked different, the way you could hear the rush and tumble of a burn, but the water was unusual, darker in the moonlight.

She said Goodnight at the road end, but he followed her up the path and over the cattle grid to the house and when Annie and Fraser went round the back, she stood awkward for a second or two, his face long and pale and shadowed and she thought she might ask him in for a cup of tea, when he said, We could go round the other side.

And she turned. She didn't say anything, because the idea had never occurred to her and she didn't know what to say, so she just turned away when he grabbed her arm and said, So you don't think I'm good enough, do you.

And while the words and the breath stuck in her throat he swung her round, hit her and ran her into the barn at the side of the house and with the cows in their stalls and the smell of the place around her he threw her onto the cemented floor and put his hand over her mouth and she kicked and pulled at his hair and face because she couldn't breathe and when at last breath came to her she took it in handfuls till she felt the pain of him inside her and she screamed, so he put his hand over her mouth but she could breathe this time, so she grabbed his hair and tugged his head back and spat at him, spat into his face, though by now he was finished and he rolled away and she put her heel into his face as he was bending forward on his hands and knees and pulling away from her. She thought she might have caught his eye for he let out a yell and grabbed her leg, but she jerked herself free and ran into the house and up the stairs and into the bathroom where she looked at herself in the mirror and though her clothes were filthy and she looked the same she knew he had changed her.

Five months later when she began to show, her mother put her on the bus to Glasgow.

The nuns took it from her. She never held the baby.

They took it while it was wet and red and dripping and the nun's apron was shining with her blood. Even though there was only a wee light bulb, she could see the red glow on the apron and hear the baby's cry.

They never told her, but she knew it was a girl.

She stayed in the hostel, working in kitchens, making soups and stews, some sandwiches and cakes to pay for her board. She never saw anyone except the nuns and the other girls: You've to hide your shame, the sister said.

Then her place was needed and with the baby gone, she was told to leave.

Of course, there's nothing to stop you going home, the sister said, but if you want to stay here we can help find you work and a place in a good, steady home.

Next morning she cleared her plate and left it on the trolley by the serving hatch, beside the teacup and plate for the toast. She collected her bag and left. She told no one she was going.

Out in the street, it was a clear, bright day. The wind was lovely, the clean, fresh smell and the feel of it full in her face, but she would have to move. She stood by the gate and the city moved around her. She knew she'd have to be quick because the van that took them to their kitchens would be leaving after the register check, when they'd find her missing, after the sister had been sent for and she'd asked if anyone knew where Catherine Morrison was and if anyone had been speaking to her. When the van left the sister would phone the police, then tell her family she was missing.

She got on a bus that said City Centre.

She was lucky. Looking back, she tells herself, she was lucky.

She got off the bus at Central Station and stood outside because she had no place to go and thought she might have to go back home.

A woman asked if she was all right and took her to the chapel house at St Bartholomew, where the woman at the door smoothed the front of her housecoat and looked down the street. You'd better come in, she said.

The house smelled of stale air freshener and polish. There was a bouquet of artificial flowers on the table beside the phone. The woman showed her into a side room.

Did you get tea? the priest asked.

I'm fine, thanks.

No, sit there and we'll fetch you in a cup of tea.

Three days later she had a place in a lodging house in Hill Street. On Sunday she went to the chapel at St Aloysius.

She wrote to Annie and told her she was settled, told her she'd got a job in the college offices and was managing fine.

Annie told her she and Fraser were engaged. She gave her the date of the wedding and told her to put it in her diary because she wanted Cathie to be her bridesmaid.

It was a hard letter to write. It took her three nights and when she'd finished it she put it straight in the envelope and phoned Annie's mobile: There's a letter in the post, she said.

I cant do it. As much as I would love to and as much as I want to and no matter what I do to try to help me make myself do it, I know I cant. It isnt you and it isnt Fraser and it isnt the wedding. You <u>must</u> know that. Who doesnt want to be at her sister's wedding. Not me, I can tell you. But I cant come home. Not yet and you know why. It's not that Im scared of who I'll see, though I dont want to see him, no its not that its just that I am not ready, not ready to come home or do anything yet. I am settling here and Im trying to settle here and its ok. Its not like home but its ok and works fine and everything. I cant write and I want to talk to you to tell you what happened and even though what happened happened she was still my baby and they took her. But I cant even talk about it, not yet. Youve to send me the pictures and tell me whats going on. You could come to Glasgow for a honeymoon though I know youve always wanted to go to Spain. Maybe you and Fraser could fly from Glasgow and I could see you then. I want to see my Daddy in a suit and tie with a flower in his lapel ready to give you away and even Mummy in a flowery hat and a new coat would be good. For God's sake Annie, <u>please, please forgive me</u> for not coming.

Her daughter would have been 18 months old when Fraser and Annie were married.

She stood on the bridge and looked at the water and

thought of what it would look like in the moonlight, though she knew this place would never be without light.

Three months later she went back for her father's funeral.

So you've come to see us, her mother said. Why weren't you here for your sister's wedding? It was a disgrace, and everyone asking where you were.

Mum. I told you about that, Annie said.

Some daughter you turned out to be, running away with your shame and thinking all you have to do is come back here to bury your father. You killed him, her mother said. He was never the same after you left.

You've no right to talk to Cathie like that, Annie said, you of all people.

She didn't speak to her mother, never said a word till after the service when the house was full of mourners.

He was there and she knew he was there. He had a scar on his forehead, running from his brow to the side of his eye.

Her mother was standing by the sideboard talking with Father McDowall and Mrs Gillies who arranged the flowers. There was an awkward hush when Cathie came into the room. She went over to Jamsie Fallon and she spat in his face.

You're not welcome here, she said. Get out.

And she turned to her mother.

Unless you invited him, of course. He can stay if he's here on your invitation.

It would be better if you left, the priest said. You can pay your respects another time James.

But he sat there, her spit drying on his face.

Annie ignored him when she went round with the tea.

Come on, Fraser said. Don't be such a dick. Get out of here. You shouldn't've bloody come in the first place.

Jamsie Fallon stood and surveyed the room. No one looked at him as he moved towards the door. He stared round the room again, turning towards his chair as if there was something he'd left.

We'll need to be going soon ourselves, Mrs Gillies said when he'd gone.

Her husband nodded.

It's getting late, a woman said.

Andy the postman stood up and looked out the window. I'll just see that everything's okay, he said.

They left as they'd arrived, trickling out in ones and twos, hugging and shaking hands.

And with everyone gone and the front room cleared, when the chairs had been put back and the extra food packed in the freezer and the sandwiches thrown in the bin for the hens, they sat round the kitchen table, the way they'd always sat, with Fraser in her father's place and Cathie facing her mother.

You'll have to come back, her mother said. Annie's going to have children and she'll have her hands full and I'm getting on, so you'll have to come back to look after me.

She never spoke, but lay in the bed where she'd slept for most of her life, staring at the ceiling, watching the way the light dimmed behind the heavy curtains, faded but did not disappear, stayed bright.

I'll look after you the way you looked after me, she said when she left next morning. She hugged her sister and kissed Fraser's cheek.

He walked her to the road end.

I'll come back to bury her, she said. And I'll send money to help pay for whatever she needs.

She might have to go into a home at the end, he said.

Then put what I send away. It'll help pay for it. I'll write a note to Annie. But if it gets too much you can let me know. We'll settle this place up when she's gone.

Things change, he said. You might want to come back and you'll surely be here to see the children. We'll see how it goes. Let us know you've got back safe.

I'll be all right, she said. God knows, I've waited here for a bus many's the time before now. You get back on up to the house.

Be sure and write, or you could phone, he said. It would be nice to hear your voice.

She waited till the sound of his boots on the gravel faded as the wind rolled over the crest of the corn, occasionally green but mostly yellow with poppies and a scattering of cornflowers, the red campion and scabious in the sheuch where she'd played. She had gathered these flowers and pressed them for a Blue Peter project, knew their names and habitation. In the afternoon the butterflies would be out and the bees would bump round the place, the swallows diving and blackbirds loud in the gloaming.

She had loved it, loved it and thought she would never leave, would marry and live here forever, bringing in the winter coal, watching the spring seeds sown, that they would carry her down the lane the way they carried her father. She and her man would maybe buy another field and get some more cows and her children would fetch them home the way she had fetched them and she would stand at the kitchen window and watch them stagger up the road in the evening.

When the bus came she sat at the back, the other seats taken in ones and twos. She knew no one and looked out the window as a chill settled inside her. It was a new feeling and it made her anxious; she knew her time here was over, not just the dream, all of it. And as she looked at her reflection in the fading light she saw herself years on, coming home from work or going to the chapel to pour the tea.

Spitting it out

She dreaded the cough that left him clawing for air. His chest let out dollops of noise and she lay there, invisible, letting him sweat and wheeze and splutter till he was done, or nearly done, when he'd lie back on the pillows and mutter.

She never tried to help him, not since he hit her and said he'd manage and told her to mind her own business. And he never spoke. One morning she said, You were bad last night, and he pressed up the television sound.

She watched him move through the house like a ghost. Everything was an effort. He sat on the bed and waited for the breath to let him stand. He didn't wash properly and took more than an hour to get dressed. He called for her to put on his socks and tie his laces; sometimes she had to button his shirt and tie his tie. His clothes looked baggy and he touched the furniture as he passed.

He stopped at the bottom of the stairs, looked to the top and tried to take a breath before going up, one stair at a time, stopping every now and then to hold onto the railing or wave his arm to find a support he knew wasn't there. When she followed him into the lavatory the water was still pink after he'd flushed the bowl. She stopped looking at his underwear.

What's the use? he said when she mentioned the doctor.

He'd stopped eating. He'd have tea and a smoke for breakfast, drink tea throughout the morning and maybe take a roll at dinner time, but he usually settled for a couple of slices of toast. He looked at food as an effort. She bought things she knew he liked, steak or a nice bit of ham, but he'd pick at the meat, then leave the rest. He'd take a drop soup, but stopped eating when he started to sweat.

Every afternoon he went to the bookie's. The journey took

between three and four hours. He never lingered. She'd watch him move along the wall, stopping every now and then to take in air, or just stand still.

And so it went for most of the summer. Then, near the end of September, after he'd eaten half a poached egg, he told his wife, I need to see her. Maybe a Sunday'd be best.

She ordered the taxi, laid out his clothes and spent the morning dressing him. The taxi came at one o'clock.

Did you tell her? he asked when they came off the motorway. And when they pulled into Margaret's street he asked again.

The taxi waited while he shuffled on the pavement in the broken glass and litter. A group of girls, quiet and aloof, stood at the corner. When the taxi pulled away, he shook his head. A minute, he said. Give me a minute. And he stood, taking the air.

Half an hour later, they were two storeys up. A wee boy opened the door and shouted, Mammy. It's a man and a woman. He walked past the child into the house.

A man in his semmit lay in bed, reading the paper. He looked up when they came in. A couple of weans were watching a video and a woman stood up from turning on a bar of the electric fire. She threw a can of super lager at the man who came in.

Not here, she said. I don't want you here. Get out. You've no right coming here. This is my house. I can do what I like. Get out.

The man jumped out of the bed and the weans cooried in behind the sofa, their eyes shut tight and their hands at their ears. The man from the bed pulled on his shirt and trousers.

Just see him, the older woman said. Just see him this time.
No.

He's your father. You have to see him. Margaret. Please.

I'm dying, he said. I know I'm dying and I need to speak to you.

The man from the bed turned him to the door and pushed him out. He fell in the lobby and as his wife tried to pull him to his feet, the younger woman fell on her knees and started punching his body. Her mother tried to stop her and the two women pulled at each other on the floor.

Look at him, her mother screamed. Look at him. He's dying.

I hope he dies. I hope he dies soon and I'll spit on his grave.

Don't, Margaret. Please. Don't say that.

You're as bad as him. You let it happen.

The children turned up the volume as the man on the lobby floor shouted, Help me. Help me stand. For God's sake, help me stand.

His wife got him to his knees. The other couple went back in to the kitchen and shut the door. He tried to grab the lobby walls but had to crawl to the door, where he gripped the handles as his wife helped him rise.

They waited for more than an hour in the rain. When the taxi came, he slumped in the back. The driver had to help her up the stairs, where she stripped and washed him down with a flannel while the bed was warmed with three hot water bottles. In a pair of crisp, newly pressed pyjamas he lay staring at the ceiling and coughed in the night, grasping air.

Do you want to tell me? she asked, when the coughing subsided. Do you want to tell me what happened with you and Margaret?

The only sound was the wheeze of his chest.

You know what I'm going to think, so tell me what happened. For God's sake.

Nothing happened, he said. It's her. She's off her head, always was and always will be.

He died three days later.

Nobody knew where he stayed and he'd no identification. The police made the betting shop staff close the shop and punters had to wait till somebody who knew him arrived two hours after he'd collapsed. By which time they'd missed four afternoon races and the ambulance had taken him to the mortuary.

Mice in the walls

He hunched into the wheel and screwed his eyes against the light, blinking to the squeak of the wipers.

Ellen asked, Is it far?

Nine, ten miles; maybe more.

Will it take long?

He didn't answer.

The heater had been on for more than two hours; as he stretched across to reduce the temperature, the car twisted and the chassis slid slightly to the right.

She grabbed his arm. He put his foot on the brake and the back of the car shifted, this time further. When it stopped they were facing the barrier at the edge of the road.

He knew the barrier would end soon, even though they would still be on the hill with falling snow, ice on the road and a sheer drop to their left.

Ellen sobbed and pulled her blanket tighter. She had been ill and wouldn't leave the car to guide him round. There was no other traffic, so it felt he could safely move backwards. He could see the verge behind, now illuminated red and white, and swung the wheel round quickly as the car moved forward.

Going downhill, Michael turned off the heating and didn't speak. Ellen pulled the blanket over her head. The fan was a distraction and he used a single wipe when the screen became blurred.

They went down slowly, in second gear, his foot on the brake, sometimes sliding when they caught a patch of ice, trembling when it suddenly stopped. The bends were difficult, especially when the car drifted to the opposite side of the road where he could hear the scrape of vegetation against his door or the main beam disappeared into the snow and sky.

He turned towards the other side of the road and waited till the beam caught something he recognised, something that told him he was still on the road and going downhill.

It took more than an hour to clear the hill.

They passed a lochan on the edge of the village, where six men were curling. An electric light above the ice divided the darkness; like something from an 18th century print, the men in bonnets, gloves and mufflers, candles in jars on the ice and their breath in the air.

He stopped the car and wound down the window, smiling at the sound of stone scraping the ice. The men passed round a hip flask, waved and he waved back.

You all right? Ellen asked.

He nodded.

Twenty minutes later she carried the last box of groceries into the kitchen while Michael fetched an armful of logs.

The coalman hasn't been, he said.

What'll we do?

I'll phone tomorrow. There's the heaters and some anthracite. It'll do for the Rayburn and we can get a bag from the shop for the other fires.

They had viewed the house in summer. The outside was painted and the garden blooming.

It's perfect, she said. Perfect.

The owner was moving south, but didn't say why or where he was going.

The estate agent admitted the house had been on the market for some time.

Property, she said. Ups and downs like everything else. What we've been saying is that there is a buyer for every house, but we like to think that because of its location and condition this is someone's dream cottage.

Absolutely, Ellen said.

Their offer was accepted immediately with a three-months entry date.

Last weekend Michael came up with the last of the books and set up his computer in the back bedroom. He went to Glasgow, helped Ellen clear the flat and this was the final move. The forecast wasn't good and they met the first of the snow outside Stirling.

The Rayburn warmed the kitchen and the heaters took the chill off the house. He lit a fire in the sitting room while Ellen made up the beds in their bedroom. They had stopped sleeping together when she took ill and somehow lost the habit.

When he had fetched the last of the logs and banked up the fire, he stood by the window and peered into the dark.

Just after nine and the fresh heat brought mice running between the walls and plaster, scrambling round the window. He remembered seeing them on the outside frame, their eyes dark, flecks of light and fire.

Flakes drifted round the window and he could make out the first of the garden trees, with a line of bushes between them and the hills. As a young man, he walked the glen and climbed the hill he was trying to see.

Ellen was too ill to walk, but hopes of doing it again brought him here.

I live here now, he thought. There's this house, then the garden with a gate to the bridge across the river and a road into the hills. There must be fish in the river, small brown trout.

And as he closed the curtains, he thought he must have seen this house as a young man, but could not remember.

The river rose with the thaw. Two fields were flooded and he thought the wooden bridge at the foot of the garden might get washed away.

The snow had settled on the roofs and was stacked in piles by the pavement edge. Traces of black ice shone along the roads and snow crystals glistered like granite, their blue light bouncing from trees and hedgerows.

Another snowfall, freezing fog and ice made the top road impassable. Their car was stuck and the post bus blocked, but he could walk to the village in rainproofs and walking boots.

The newspapers and magazines they ordered often arrived days late, so he usually went down to the village in the early afternoon, after the post bus had been, and took to delivering letters and parcels on his way back uphill.

Their days had a pattern. Michael worked after breakfast, they usually had soup for lunch and Ellen slept when he went to the village. He knew she slept, but never said. There was comfort in the fact that she could choose when she should sleep. It meant she was getting better, not quite restored, but better. The move and its changes had definitely helped.

There was a bouncy reassurance in the way the consultant outlined his proposals. His voice had the edge of a salesman, someone who had gone over the options too often, who anticipated questions and saw their danger. An operation would be difficult because of where the tumour lay; chemotherapy and radiation should do the trick.

It didn't.

When Ellen was at her weakest, he told them the tumour had grown and surgery was the only option.

He hadn't finished speaking when Ellen said, I'll do it.

Don't you want to think about it, discuss the options?

If I've understood you, there are no options.

For days she hadn't smelled like herself, too many drugs and morphine and he was sure she would die. The day before the operation she asked him not to come. He went to the cinema twice and could not remember what he had seen.

She was 12 hours in theatre and he saw her 30 hours after the operation. Her hair was combed. She had put on eye shadow and lipstick. But the smell was still there.

I've asked them if they think I am going to die to phone you. I don't want to die alone, she said.

Insofar as we can tell, the consultant said nine months later, you're clear. No guarantees, of course, but it's better, much better than we expected.

It took her twenty minutes to climb the stairs to the flat. We have to move, she said. And when they closed the front door, she crumbled on to the floor and cried.

I never thought I'd see this place again, she said.

They had New Year in Glasgow. The walls were bare and the carpets rolled. The remaining furniture was draped in dust covers, like a stage set for someone returning to a cold and uninhabited house. Only the kitchen resembled itself even though the cupboards were empty and their food was in boxes.

They toasted the year in sherry with Sandy and Alex, their neighbours of more than 20 years.

It'll be strange with new people here, Alex said. God knows what we're going to get. I hope we can find something to talk about apart from factor's bills and the stair cleaning.

We might not be here too long ourselves, said Sandy. This place is not what it was.

On the last day, Ellen went from room to room, running her finger along the walls. When she had closed the door she clutched the keys tightly before slipping them through the letterbox.

When he came back with the letters, he could see she wasn't long up. Her eyelids were heavy, the bits around the eyes and cheeks were softer and her walk was cautious, like a spaceman.

He took off his boots and put their post on the table.

Ellen boiled a kettle and gave him a row about walking around in stocking feet. Michael found his slippers and switched on the computer.

Seen this? she said.

In the 10 days between the previous owner leaving and their arrival, the phone had been used to call America, New

Zealand and Turkey.

Michael took the tea she made and left to check his emails. He got compassionate leave when Ellen was ill; when he told them about the move, they suggested a short-term contract.

He liked the time alone, often staring out the window to the hill at the back, imagining what the trees, the hill, the burn and rocks would be like in summer, enjoying the reassuring sounds from the kitchen, the radio, the clatter of pans and crockery, sometimes leaving early to ask if there was anything he could do to help. It mostly involved setting the table and pouring wine.

Do you think someone came here and used the phone? she asked, reaching for the salt.

I don't know. I suppose it's possible. We should check the bill before jumping to conclusions. What we can do is tell them the calls aren't ours. We can prove we weren't here. The calls were made before our move-in date.

The silence as they finished their meal stressed how important he had become. Ellen depended on him. She had found it difficult to settle, to adjust to the new way of life. She had talked about joining the quilting class, going to cookery demonstrations or helping out at the playgroup, always adding, When I'm feeling better.

They had a dishwasher, but Michael did the washing-up. He was at the sink when Ellen said she fancied an early night.

I've left a list on the table, if you're still going tomorrow, she said.

I'll see what the weather's like.

Michael finished the wine, watched the end of Mastermind and read in front of the sitting room fire. He loved this time, when Ellen was in bed and he was alone with the wind and the shifting snow on the roof, the mice in the walls and the fall of the fire.

Reading was one of the things he most looked forward to, a memory from his childhood and teenage years when he lost himself in books. He imagined he would be able to do so again, but hadn't read as much as he liked.

He had hoped to build reading time into his day, like answering emails and walking to the Post Office. But days were often determined by Ellen's mood or condition. The library van came on Thursday afternoons and he often handed books back without finishing or sometimes opening them.

He avoided the hill, going through the Bottom End of the village, a bit he didn't know. He left just after 10 and had the shopping finished by one o'clock. He had pie and chips in the supermarket café and started back some time before two.

There was a diversion.

Bad accident, the policeman said. It's the weather. You'll need to be careful.

When the policeman had guided him round, told him to follow the yellow diversion signs and wished him well, the trickle of snowflakes onto the windscreen reminded him of the way cherry blossom petals swirled in spring. The sky was coloured charcoal and slate.

The diversion added more than twenty miles to his journey and the road was busy. There were no passing places or lay-bys, so he could not phone and knew she would be worried. He wound down a window to clear the air and caught the slur of tyres in the slush.

He saw the boy on the edge of the village and coming into the Bottom End felt the snap across the windscreen. In his mind, the boy was still, arm in the air, a smile on his face, having thrown the snowball and caught his target, a better throw than he expected.

There must have been a stone in the snowball. The crack radiated across the screen, like ice on a pond.

The car skidded awkwardly across the road. The boy hadn't moved; owlish, with short dark hair and a high forehead, he stood by the side of the road, staring.

Michael had him by the arm and was shaking him, screaming.

What's your name? Tell me your name.

He stopped when he realised what he was doing and the boy shook himself free.

Fuck off, he said and turned.

Michael grabbed him again.

Where do you live? Where's your father?

The boy spat in Michael's face.

Just fuck off.

Michael wiped his face with a handkerchief and watched the boy run into the woods.

When he brought in the shopping, Ellen was sitting in the dark.

I thought you were dead, she said. I thought you'd gone over the hill.

He took her hand. Why didn't you phone? he asked.

I couldn't. I didn't want to know. If you were driving you couldn't answer.

Have you eaten?

She shook her head.

They'll know who you are, she said, and the father will come looking. What will you do if he asks, Did you hit my boy? This is a funny place. He won't repair your windscreen. You'll have to pay for that yourself and no one will talk to me. The men in the pub will move when you come in. No one will speak and you'll have to walk up the road on your own.

And with that he realised Ellen had changed, like a dog with too many owners, a dog that has been passed from one to the other and after time will leave having formed no attachment.

Outside, snow was falling. Michael put on his coat and stood in the garden facing the hill, listening to the river trickling through ice.

Korsakoff's Psychosis

He who fights with monsters might take care least he thereby become a monster. And if you gaze for long into an abyss, the abyss gazes also into you.

Jenseits von Gut und Böse, IV, 146.

Friederich Nietzsche (1844-1900)

1

I turned the corner and there he was, puffed and bloated with a slight taste of kitchen grease, his clothes dishevelled, the smell of sweat still in the fabric.

How's it going?

Okay.

It's been a while.

Yeah. I've been busy.

Still doing meetings?

Not really, maybe the odd one, nothing regular.

He drew his hand across the stubble and shifted his weight.

How's, ehm, whatshisname?

Eddie?

No, the other guy.

Andy?

Yeah, Andy.

Which one?

There was an ache in his eyes and he tried a smile.

I have to go, he said. Tell Andy I was asking for him.

I'd seen him around, but we hadn't really spoken till he pulled me away from the others and asked for help.

I need to stop, he said, as if it was something I could do for him.

But when I called he'd change the subject, usually to talk about Jennifer.

Then nothing till I heard she was gone and he was in a treatment centre. She'd been around as long as I'd known him, a presence. By the time we met in the park there were things he didn't know, or I thought he didn't know, about Jennifer and me.

She phoned, late, just after he went into treatment.

I hope you don't mind me calling.

Is it about Derek?

He wants to come home.

And how do you feel?

I don't know. I think he should stay, but he says it's awful, like being in the army, very strict. He has to get up at six, has to cook for everybody and chop wood.

Not every day.

No, I understand all that team spirit stuff. But he has to write things about his mother and father, his boss and me and he's not very good at introspection.

I don't know much about Derek. I know about his drinking and that's it.

He's an architect and could make good money, but he isn't working. Guess why.

Did he ask you to phone?

No. It was my idea. He doesn't know I've phoned. And don't tell him. He'd hate it.

I'm not going to lie.

Maybe I've done the wrong thing. I'm sorry.

I spoke to male alcoholics every day, many times a day and they never apologised for taking my time; this detached, impersonal *viva voce* was unusual.

What were you hoping to get; I mean, why did you phone?

Derek spoke about you, he mentioned your name quite a lot actually and I took the number from a notebook. It was a spur of the moment thing. I thought you'd be able to help, tell me what was going on, what it's all about. Why does he have to write stuff? Apparently there's a place for wives. I won't have to go there, will I?

Not if you don't want to, but you would be talking to people in the same position as yourself.

There was a pause, mostly silence; once or twice a sound that could have been the start of a cough or a sentence, but otherwise nothing. She began slowly.

He wants to get better. Or says he does. It's difficult to tell what he wants. One minute he's talking about remortgaging the house and starting a new business, the next minute he doesn't want to stay because he has to write stuff.

Maybe what he wants is to drink with safety.

And that won't happen?

What do you think? Vested interests will tell you otherwise, but I've never seen anyone take the road back to social drinking. The illusion kills people, drives them mad. At best you have a half-life, stopping and starting, waiting for the next bout, or you effectively stop and would be as well not drinking at all, though you do have to deal with your feelings and your past.

I looked out on the winding ribbon of yellow light, the traffic going home. The only sound was her breathing. I started speaking with no idea of where the thought would end, to try to paste over the gaps.

He has to write things to understand what's going on, so he can begin to see he's not the victim of misfortune or circumstance, that he actually has a say in these matters, there are choices and decisions. But none of this is going to work unless he can see the point of doing it. And even then it might not work. If Derek decides to drink again, nothing will stop him, and it sounds as if you're not convinced he wants to stop. The initial thrust has to come from him. He has to want to stop.

Do you think I should let him come home?

I'm sorry. I can't make that decision for you.

What did your wife do?

I didn't have a wife.

I thought you were married?

Not in the beginning, not when I came in and not now.

Oh, I'm sorry. It's just that, I wondered, but it's probably no good asking.

What did you wonder?

Will you go and see him?

I was thinking about it.

When?

The weekend. There's a Sunday meeting. I'll take him to that.

When I walked into the common room he was staring out the window, across the lawn and shrubbed edges down to the river. It was raining. He'd been watching the door and turned away when he saw me, affecting preoccupation.

Oh, hi, he said.

I gave him cigarettes and we walked to the coffee urn.

How's things?

Terrible. Jenni thinks I should stay. I don't suppose she's phoned you?

He couldn't tell me how long he'd been there and was not interested in how long he'd been sober.

All that counting days stuff; what's the point. One day's the same as the next. And before you ask I'm clean as well, tobacco in my lungs and nothing up my nose.

So, how's it going, apart from the terrible bits?

It's all terrible.

Do you want to talk about it?

Not really. I want to go home.

They won't keep you. If you want to leave, you should have a word with them. I'm going to the meeting. Fancy it?

He sighed, looked round the room.

I'm going out for a smoke, he said.

When he thought about it, and he didn't like to think about it, but every now and then something forced him to consider the possibility that he was in the right place. He could be like the others, not only because he drank in the same ways they did and for pretty much the same reasons, nor because of their shared experience, but because someone dropped the idea that he thought and felt the way they did.

Everybody told him. Three doctors and his lawyer; Jennifer had told him many times, her lawyer told him; every boss he'd worked for told him; his neighbours told him; his mother and Jennifer's mother persisted in telling him; his father, his sister, his brother and his sister's man and their children told him; his brother's wife in Canada whom he had never met wrote and told him; the police told him many times; three sheriffs, two judges and God knows how many nurses and medical orderlies told him; and one Saturday afternoon a wee woman in a woollen hat and slippers standing in the Tesco queue told him: Jesus Christ, she said, have a look at yourself, you're as pished as a lavvy wall.

I didn't enjoy the meeting. It disturbed me how quickly I had slipped through the Jennifer question. The chairman asked Derek if he had anything to say. He shook his head and stared out the window till the meeting was over. Then he made for the door. I squeezed in front, stood in his way, then steered him towards a side entrance.

Let's take a turn round the grounds, I said, get some air.

I told him I used to be sorry for the folk who needed this stuff, wished them well, maybe even wanted to help them, but none of it applied to me. Or maybe some of it did; little bits here and there, but nothing like all of it. I was different, I knew what I was doing and could stop any time, any time at all. The first time we get this, it's a gift. After that, we've got to work for it, which means it's harder.

That's pish, he said. Gifts, serenity, spirituality, all of that indefinable, unquantifiable drivel; it's just words.

He stopped and faced me, trembling slightly. His eyes were

watery, he had his hands in his pockets and he shifted his weight from foot to foot like a boxer. I was going to say something about taking a turn down by the river, walking along the path and getting back in time for tea, that it would be easier if we kept going, when he suddenly turned: You trying to scare me? he said.

I don't think that's possible. I think you think you're different. You think this is temporary?

It is temporary. You don't think I'll stay here, do you?

That's not what I mean and you know it.

He turned, crashing through the rhododendrons and Japanese knotweed. When I grabbed his arm he shook himself free.

You'll leave because you don't want to stop drinking. You want rid of the shakes and the fear and the sweats and the blackouts. But you're still holding on to the crazy idea, you think there's a way out. You think you'll get a pill or an injection or you'll be brainwashed into drinking normally. Doesn't happen. I'm sorry, but it doesn't happen.

He stopped and turned, his fists clenched, body stretched and tense, his head back, shouting at the sky: How do you know?

For the same reason you know, because the compulsion stays and the stuff that makes you drink is still there, and unless you find a way of dealing with that and the way you feel about yourself there's no road back to normality, not for you, not for me, not for anyone.

But some folk can do it.

I've never met them.

That's because you don't know everyone who's tried. It'll happen, even though you wouldn't expect it.

Like falling asleep in a dentist's chair?

He lit a cigarette and turned away, blowing his smoke into the wind.

Bet you could do with a drink right now? I said.

He laughed.

But you've proved you don't need it. So we're dealing with

an obsession.

Don't start that stuff, allergy, obsession. Jesus, you don't even know what these words mean. Has anybody ever told you how pompous you sound?

He'd stopped shouting and was talking slowly with long pauses before speaking, as though he was looking for a response, measuring what his reaction should be. It gave his answers a determined quality, though his voice was now soft and he smiled occasionally. He seemed to be enjoying himself.

He was thinner than me, his teeth were straight, he looked healthier, he was tanned and better dressed. We must have made an odd looking pair, him tall, dark and razor-like, his hair damp and silver: then me, skinny, awkward, dandruff on my shoulders.

Is it a class thing?

He turned to look at me and flicked the cigarette into the wet grass, where I thought I heard it hiss.

What?

Do you think you're better than them? That it won't happen to you because it only happens to stupid people, plodders who have no self-control, no will power, who have lost the ability to stay within their limit and never had a choice in the first place. Final question. Did you ask Jennifer to phone me?

No, he said. And he turned back up the path and straight into the common room, where Jennifer was standing by the coffee urn, beneath the 'Take Life One Day at a Time' sunset poster.

She was not the woman I'd imagined. Her voice had been husky and concerned. Maybe she'd been crying before she phoned and certainly found the conversation difficult. This woman's hair was long. She wore stiletto heels, a black coat and maroon sweater with a brooch at her throat. She had a bag with a thin dark strap over her shoulder and was standing with her legs slightly apart, her weight on one hip. She had freshly poured coffee in a Styrofoam cup and was holding a packet of cigarettes.

I didn't think you were coming, he said.

She smiled and looked at me, which caused him to affect a casual introduction, immediately asking, almost as part of the same sentence, Where's the car?

I came by bus.

Why?

You know I hate driving in the rain.

How are you getting home?

Bus. How are you doing?

If you'd brought the car you could've taken me home.

Derek looked at me.

I'll get off, I said.

No one answered.

Did you see the doctor?

Uh-huh.

Did he say you could go home?

Have you any cigarettes?

They walked to the door.

Listen, I said. I'd best go.

Thanks, she said, for coming here. Thanks.

Tell me about it, the doctor said, leaning across the desk, hands together.

Still he doesn't answer.

Well, let me tell you. It might be the next time, it might be the time after. It might be sudden or it could take a while. It might leave you in a permanent vegetative state or it could be partial, which means you'll be slavering and incontinent. You with me? You're sure you're following this?

He nods.

On the other hand, it could be none of these things. It could be something else, something new, but it will be recognisable because the thing that makes it difficult to predict is you. It has a different effect on different people.

What you're saying is you don't know?

No. The doctor sighs and looks at him. What I'm saying is I do know. What I'm saying is I know it will happen. That's why we do brain scans. I know it will happen, but I don't know when. And I don't know the form it'll take when it does happen. I know you're at risk and I'm telling you what that risk is; I'm saying if you carry on doing what you're doing, drinking the way you're drinking and battering into other stuff as well, whatever's going, then it'll happen. Nothing surer. I'm saying you've no control. I'm saying you've lost control, if, indeed, you ever had it. I am saying you cannot control your drinking and therefore have no choice.

But you don't really know, do you? If you don't know when it'll happen or what it'll be, what do you know?

The doctor's fed up with this. I know it'll happen, he says.

Then I'll control it, cut it down. Take vitamin B.

If you could've done that, you wouldn't be here.

I'll stop before it gets too bad.

No you won't. That's what I'm trying to tell you; you've no say in the matter. Once you start, you're compelled to continue.

I have to stop sometime.

And by then it could be too late. The trick is not to start. The trick is to stop and stay stopped.

I don't need to stop. I need to control it.

But you can't control it.

I'm fed up with this.

Me too.

I've been here, I don't know, two, nearly three weeks and I don't feel any better. This isn't working. I want to go home.

I flashed the lights and she ran towards the car.

I'm glad you waited, she said. I hoped you would. I didn't want to phone again. Do you mind if I smoke? I'll roll down the window.

I'd prefer it if you didn't smoke in the car.

She put the cigarette back in the packet and the packet in her bag, folded her hands across her lap and stared straight ahead.

Did he see the doctor?

She nodded and told me the story.

He's going to leave. There's not much more I can do. Things aren't great between us; what do you expect? The tension, rows, smashing things around the house and you might as well know this, I don't suppose he's told you, but he watches stuff on his computer, young women, teenagers. It's disgusting. And he thinks he's coming home and we're going to carry on, same as before, trying to make things work, but that's not going to happen, not when he's drinking and he's going to drink again, nothing surer. Yet he goes on denying it. I know what to do, he says. I can control it.

She fumbled in her bag and tore open a fresh packet of tissues, then stared at the road ahead, dabbing her eyes, blowing her nose and ripping the tissue into fragments she piled on her lap.

He's going to turn up at the door. I know he is. I can feel it. He does that all the time, ever since I've known him. He hijacks the agenda. Last week he was on about a second mortgage and opening a coffee shop. It's lunacy. We can't even pay the mortgage we've got. When he mentioned the coffee shop, I said I thought he should get himself settled, see how things were working and maybe get a job. His old boss would take him back, if he was sober. I know he would. As soon as I spoke he started going on about dark green walls with natural pine tables and cork flooring, etchings or really bright pictures, vibrant colours on the walls, selling coffee cheaper than anyone else. It was as if he hadn't heard me, but he'd heard me all right. He didn't like what I said, so he went back to his dream. It's real enough to him. I bet he's redecorated this imaginary place four or five times since he's been in there.

I stopped for petrol. It was dearer than the city, but I wanted out the car. I filled the tank, looked at the remains of the Sunday papers and paid the girl.

Some night, she said. And the forecast isn't good. Are you going far?

Glasgow.

I finish in 10 minutes and I hope my lift turns up.

There were two screens above her, repeating images of the courtyard and soundless ITV. I couldn't see Jennifer.

She was standing by the door smoking. She had been crying and emptied the tissue pieces one by one into the night. Back in the car, she sighed.

And there's his mother, she said, trying to laugh. God, it's pathetic. Last time she phoned she told me he was all right till he met me. He was a clever boy, she said, always good at school. His trouble was he got married too soon: Nothing to do with you, dear, I'm not saying that, but he doesn't have a family. I mean, there's no children.

She touched my hand, suddenly withdrew and didn't speak till we reached the city.

Stop here, she said.

Carlo's Fish, Chips and Pizza.

Are you hungry?

I haven't had a proper meal in ages. Scrambled eggs, toast and banana, coffee and cigarettes.

How about something to eat?

And I immediately regretted it. This was too familiar.

Where?

I don't know, but I'm sure we could do better than Carlo's.

Actually, I should go home, but I couldn't face another night on my own.

Do you know the China Bazaar?

I think so.

Let's go there. It's quick.

I thought we'd ordered too much, fried rice, Singapore

noodles, beef and ginger, chicken kung po, prawns and watercress, but she worked her way through everything, smiling when I'd finished as she helped herself to the last of the beef and rice.

I think you'll have to carry me, she said.

The rain had stopped. But the air was damp and by the time we reached the car our faces were wet.

I told her I lived on a hill above the park and often walked there after rain.

It's the smell, she said, the fresh, clean smell. Let's do it. Let's walk through the park.

I parked in the basement bay and we walked to the gate, where she took off her shoes and took my arm as we went into the dark.

She talked all the time, about the ten years, maybe eleven since she came to Glasgow, about a shared flat, three other girls and her job temping where she met Alan, Derek's ex-boss, who offered her a job.

He was married and I thought, well, you know what I thought. It was on and off for ages, till Derek and I started seeing each other. No one knew. It was very hush-hush. When Derek asked me out, I was flattered. Alan was furious. I don't think he's forgiven me.

Do you still see him?

Not really, now and then. I left when I got married and we didn't speak for ages. I avoided all the office dos, but had to phone when Derek couldn't make it and give all sorts of excuses. One day the receptionist said, Mr. Grant wants to speak to you. He wanted to see me. What could I do? Derek wasn't sacked, he left, had a row with a client and came home. I'm not going back, he said. Alan used to phone and Derek wouldn't speak to him. I thought he must have got wind of things, but he's never known. Hasn't a clue. I went back temping. Alan and I used to meet in the afternoon, when Derek thought I was at work. I'm cold. Take me back.

It was like theatrical timing, the way the stage suddenly

darkens, the flash of light, noises off. As soon as she finished speaking the rain came. Not just a dribble, but a full downpour, the kind you can watch cross the horizon like light from a hill or an open plain.

She was shivering when we got to the car.

If you haven't any whisky, tea'll do, she said.

The time will come, maybe years from now, when none of this will matter, when individuals will tell it differently, if they tell it at all. Most likely, folk will remember someone else's actions rather than their own, their participation will have changed, but the main thrust, the energy, the anger and deceit will have faded.

I'm not clear what happened. I don't remember a sequence. I wakened in the night and stared at the ceiling, wondering if I would believe what happened.

Nothing happened.

She stretched across the floor and lit a cigarette. Now what do we do?

This must have been around two. We'd talked about her finding help for herself, had drunk lots of tea and were tired.

Can you give me money for a taxi?

Yes. Or I could take you.

Or I could stay.

I don't think that's a good idea.

Probably not, but I don't know what I want. If it makes things any easier, I don't love Derek. Put it this way, if I did I can't remember. And he needs you. Right now he needs you more than anyone. And I think I need you too.

I slept on the sofa. Others had said how comfortable it was. Now I knew they were lying.

We slept late.

I can't imagine not knowing you this time yesterday, she said.

We were having breakfast in the kitchen. The phone rang.

I'm leaving, he said. Today if I can arrange it. I can't get hold of Jenni. I don't know where she is, but she didn't go home last night. She'll be with my ex-boss. She's been shagging him for years, thinks I don't know.

She was staring at me.

He's coming home. Today if he can manage.

Right, she said. That's that. Settled.

I stood in the sitting room and stared across the city, watching a plane tremble into land.

I have to get back to my place, she said. I'll phone him from there. He hasn't keys and I'm going to change the locks. Alan and his wife are off to the States. He says it's business, but I don't believe him. He needs somebody to look after the flat. He gave me the keys and said I could stay. But I think I've just volunteered Derek.

She stopped at the door.

Has he said anything about me and Alan?

I didn't respond.

And I suppose he knows I wasn't home last night? By the way, your poker face is funny and doesn't work. He'll have phoned the bloody house every ten minutes till three or four o'clock.

Did he see you get into the car?

He was with the nurse when I left, getting medication. He didn't see me. Don't make this any more complicated than it already is. I'll phone you later. Will you be here?

Should be.

And what are you going to do?

Work.

I was still by the window in my dressing gown when we hugged and she kissed my cheek.

Derek needed to see me immediately. He was going to a meeting and hoped I'd be there. Jennifer left a mobile number.

Mission accomplished, she said. What are you doing, and are you going to have a long boy chat afterwards?

I don't know. It's possible, but unlikely. We've never had a long chat.

He's at the flat tonight and is moving into Alan's place tomorrow. A guy from the estate agent's is coming up to tell us how much our place is worth, then it's going on the market. I thought I might stay with you, if that's all right.

I know the signs, he said, as sure as I know my own name. She's met someone. I know it. It's a new thing, sudden, something that's happened quickly. It isn't you, is it?

I didn't expect the question and missed the response.

Oh for fucksake. Thanks for that, pal. Thanks for your fucken help.

Wait a minute. Hold on. Nothing's happened.

Oh sure.

She stayed at my place last night.

Because she was scared and didn't want to be alone?

She slept on the bed and I slept on the couch.

And I'm supposed to believe that?

You can believe what you like. You seem to believe you can drink with safety. This is more reasonable and it actually happened. As I understand it, your wife has told you she wants a divorce. She's put your house on the market and you're worried about an affair you think she's having. You're going to have to ask yourself, what are you going to do?

Alan isn't going to the States, by the way. He's at home, working. His wife's gone to the States, which means I can't have the flat.

Where are you staying?

With my mother, any chance of a lift?

Her skin was as pale as the wallpaper. She was surrounded by roses, on the furniture, walls and teacups.

If you ask me, he never should have married. Not that I'm biased and I certainly don't believe in class distinction or anything like that, though I do believe in merit, but she was rather a common girl. Have you met her?

Briefly.

Then you'll know what I mean. And I know for a fact, I know better than anyone, Derek was never like this before he met her. He never drank nearly as much. And he certainly didn't need to go to a clinic. I'd have liked them to have children. But she didn't want that. A man changes when he has children. Stands to reason. He has a family to consider.

I got home about eleven and went to bed at one. Jennifer hadn't appeared and didn't phone.

You should have called me, she said. Oh, you should have phoned. I wish you'd phoned. I fell asleep. I was exhausted. I sat down to watch television and the next thing I know it's morning. I can't remember going to bed. How did you get on?

She had spoken to Derek. He seemed all right, wanted a bigger share of the house sale because he'd put more money into it. And his architectural and design expertise enhanced the value of the property, especially in the kitchen and bathroom.

Where are you?

Home. I'm waiting on the estate agent. Should have been here half an hour ago. What are you doing tonight?

Nothing.

Why don't I get some stuff and cook us a meal. What time will you be in?

I don't know. Four, half four.

Expect me around six.

She was waiting when I got home, sitting on the steps outside the main entrance, reading a newspaper.

Oh, look at you, she said, coming in from work. You look great. I got some prawns, which I know you like because you, greedy pig, ate them all in China Bazaar. And I thought I'd do a pasta thing with a creamy sauce and fried leeks.

Sounds fine.

Come and talk to me. Did you miss me?

I'd be lying if I said I didn't think about you.

Did it surprise you?

Not really. I half expected it. I was looking forward to seeing you, as well as getting my tea cooked.

Did it ever occur to you that I might feel like that? she said. Did you never think I might have missed you? What's going on, or what do you imagine is going on?

I don't know. And that's the problem. I don't know what's going on.

With whom?

Anyone. I don't know what's happening. I'm constantly being wrong-footed. First I hear one thing, then another. I don't know what to believe.

We went to the cinema, to a costume drama about a woman who lets a man take the credit for her work.

Why did she do that? Jennifer said the first time it happened.

She is the only person I have known to leave the cinema in the middle of the film to have a cigarette. When she came back her phone had shifted from the top of her bag to her pocket.

So, a pattern was established. She'd come and go, sometimes arriving or leaving in the middle of the night. She'd come round, bring a change of clothes and read by the fire, watch television or have a bath. She'd cook and bake, make soup, do crosswords, knit, sew, start and finish jigsaws, play patience. She would talk for hours about nothing or sit by the window, staring at the rain.

Sometimes she would sleep in the chair and be gone in the morning. Or she'd arrive and say, I'm not staying, and still be around two days later. Or, all of a sudden, in the middle of something, she would rise and leave. Sometimes she came round for a meal and left immediately after. Sometimes she turned up in the morning and at least twice appeared late at night in the rain.

I've been for a walk, she said.

I saw her one night in town near a gay nightclub, a taxi drew up. A guy in make-up, wig, pink tights and tutu paid the driver, opened the backdoor and escorted her out. She ran upstairs.

Don't forget your wand, the driver said.

The man reached in the back and produced a pink umbrella, which he waved at the driver.

Turn to shite, he said, and followed Jennifer up the stairs.

The doorman told me I would have to join. It cost £300 and there's an eighteen months waiting list.

I'm here to see someone who's just come in. A friend.

That's what they all say.

Her mobile was usually switched off. Once or twice, when I did get through, she said, I'll call you back, and hung up.

She told me she was staying at the flat, dealing with viewings and haggling with the estate agent. She didn't know what she was going to do, was worried, had looked at other places but could afford nothing in the area. One and two bedroom flats were snapped up quickly.

Derek had moved into Alan's flat. His mother phoned on the first night to see if he needed anything and told him she could call in anytime, she was coming into town anyway.

And Alan had arranged an overdue back payment.

No idea how much, could be okay.

Did you know about it?

Sort of, but he mentioned it when we were discussing the flat, said he'd take the rent from the money I was due.

I asked if he'd seen her, if he knew where she was or if she'd been in contact.

She's seeing someone. You are apparently a friend, that's all, but she's said that before. She's had a number of friends. As far as we're concerned, her and me, it's over. I know that. I reckon she's hanging round waiting for Alan to come back before deciding what to do. This guy, whoever he is, is spare. His job is to stop her feeling lonely.

Days passed. I wandered through the park, hoping she'd be there when I got home. I left messages and answered immediately when the phone rang. I couldn't sleep and sat at the window, listening to something or other, watching grey light seep across the city sky.

Then, something like a week, eight days after I'd seen him, Derek phoned. He'd gone to the police. They told him there was nothing they could do, unless he listed his wife as a missing person.

And two nights later he turned up at the door.

She's going to London, he said. She's definitely going to London. The estate agent asked if I was going to London with my wife. And Alan's in London. He's setting up a practice there and she's joining him. I phoned the office and they told me. I asked if he was in America and they said he was in London.

Look, this can't go on.

What?

The reason we got involved was because I was supposed to be trying to help and now I'm someone who talks to you about your wife and what she's doing, someone who listens to your complaints about how awful life is, who knows you're biding your time and will drink at the first excuse, rather than opportunity. When were you last at a meeting?

Fuck you and your meetings. You don't know, you do not know what's real and what isn't. And you don't know what I'm dealing with here. You think you do, but you don't. I've tried to tell you, but you don't understand. For all I know, you could be this other guy Jenni's seeing. You could be. I'm not saying you are, but you could be seeing her and seeing me and trying to keep both ends happy. You certainly seem remote, man. Not interested in me. All you ask is if I've been to a meeting.

Come here.

I stretched my arms towards him and he came in. He wrapped his arms around me and cried, small sobs that could have been a cough, then he moaned, like a wounded animal, the way a dog yells when it's been run over or beaten into submission, when its life has gone.

He pulled away, looked at me, shrugged and left. And apart from the time when we met in the park, I never saw him again.

2

They dropped the price twice, but the house wasn't sold. He was expecting Alan's money and tried to borrow on the strength of it, did the usual rounds, but no one believed him, so he went to his mother.

I imagine she listened with the detached and silent fear of a woman whose son has shamed her many times, but who still wants to believe him; a woman who cannot accept the evidence that presents itself every time she sees him. She and her husband had done their best, scrimped, scraped and sacrificed, but Derek never should have married.

He hated the way she turned her back and hunched her shoulders when she looked in her purse, the way she counted her money before giving; but she gave it to save him humiliation, knowing he had already asked anyone he thought could help, that he was beyond embarrassment.

What about the house sale?

He'd tell her it was coming along. And he was due money from his last job, a back payment.

Maybe you should put some of it away.

She had no idea why she said this, other than the persistence of a repeated idea; she knew the symptoms better than he did and knew the consequence as well.

Yeah. If I don't get another place right away, I'll do that, he said.

And they knew he wouldn't, knew he could not be trusted with money, especially what he'd get from the sale of the house.

Anyway. One fine day, he's in the hall in Alan's flat, walking up and down and up and down, from the door to the kitchen, from the kitchen to the door when he hears the click of the letterbox. He runs, runs to the post and falls on his knees. There it is.

The brown envelope.

Imagine your most precious moment, the birth of a child or the orgasm you feared, scoring the winning goal in a World Cup final two minutes from time; all in one, and it doesn't come close.

It's a smile.

It isn't punching the air, clenching your fist or any of that. It's a slow smile. It's saying thank you to the God you don't believe in for getting it right.

I've no idea how much he got – three, four grand something like that. Maybe more. Can you even begin to imagine the feeling? Can't you catch something of it now as it brushes past your cheek? That morning, he'd been wondering where his wife was, who she was with, he'd been worrying what to do and fearing the worst, that whatever he did would confirm his worst misgivings. And now he is three, four or five thousand pounds richer, which immediately makes him something he's not.

Now he could become a new person with a nice new life. And if, by chance, he happened to meet his wife, he would meet her as a new person, newly dressed and clothed. He could impress her by presenting himself as someone else, could offer a new image as someone who is doing well without her.

He found a barber, a proper barber who not only shaved and powdered his face, but shampooed and cut his hair. He gave him a £20 tip, thought about it, looked in the mirror, ran his hand across his face and gave the guy another tenner.

Then he went shopping.

Imagine you're a bird or an angel looking down on Buchanan Street. And there he is, running from shop to shop, collecting carrier bags then a taxi back to the flat where he showers and changes. He's tried everything, from Armani to Zenga, eventually settling on Hugo Boss. He got a shirt and tie in one shop, the suit in another, shoes, raincoat and so on, paying cash each time. And now he's converted he has to see the woman who wants him to impress her.

You be careful, she'll say.

But she always says that. From the time he was a toddler and banged his head on the dresser, whenever he made for the door on his own, she'd tell him, You be careful.

A television murmurs in the sitting room.

Are you sure you can afford it?

He nods.

It's a lot of money. I wouldn't want you to leave yourself short.

He smiles and looks at his new watch. It's fine, he says. Honestly. It's fine.

She mentions the house, but that's still to come.

He's got to rush. He doesn't want to linger. He'd done what he set out to do.

She offers food. He shakes his head. I'll be eating later, he says.

I'll be making it for myself anyway.

No, you're fine, he says.

I've got a wee chop. It'll only take a minute.

No. I'm going to phone a taxi.

In the cab he thought about eating, but decided against it. He wasn't hungry. He'd catch something later.

Imagine a wine bar, a real wine bar, crowded with people.

And already there are spaces between the bits he remembers. But this, he reckons, has nothing to do with the sequence of events. It has to do with the gaps, the anticipation.

He told the taxi driver to stop at an off-licence. He got out and bought a half-bottle of whisky to catch up with himself. He has this idea that when he gets to whereever he's going everyone will have had a few drinks and he doesn't want to get there sober.

Next thing he knows, or the next thing he can remember, he is buying drinks and entertaining three or four women. This is what he wants. If only she could see him now. This is why he took the half-bottle, to feel the way everyone else looks. To walk into a room, any room, and feel confident, to talk to people the way he is talking to these women. They like him. Everybody likes him. The women smile and the bar staff smile. They act as if they've known him all their lives, touch him in a caring way, brush nothing from his jacket, play with his fingers, fiddle with his lapel while he's talking; they fix his hair and when they want a drink they look across the rim of the glass and call him darling.

Then someone has a wonderful idea. Let's go to Bozos.

So they move to a club where they waltz through security, introduce him to everyone, order champagne and while he's paying, talk with their friends, join a larger group by the bar.

He doesn't like it. He's no longer the centre of attention. They're beginning to take him for granted.

But he's fine, he knows how to handle this, keep cool, don't panic, whatever you do, don't panic and don't let them know how you feel.

They're discussing something that happened when he wasn't there, and they're not including him, filling each other in with their part of the story. One of the girls shouts, Drinks, darling. And he ignores her, but she orders it anyway and when the barman approaches he has to break another fifty and doesn't know how much he's got left. But there'll be plenty. He started off with thousands. There'll be plenty. But he knows he can't be trusted, knows where that's got him in the past. He knows it's best to wait. See what happens.

Suddenly the dealer says, Hi. And doesn't hang around.

Can I help anyone? he asks with a smile. Nice teeth. Slicked back hair. Looks like a salesman, some sort of businessman, stares at you long enough to know. They don't nod. They tell him with their eyes.

He follows the dealer into the lavatory and does a line, then does three or four lines rapid. When drink doesn't work or stops working or isn't working fast enough, this works. And the more he has the more he wants. He'll never get enough. But the dealer knocks him back.

One more.

Sorry.

How much?

You've had too much already.

What the fuck are you, a dealer with a conscience? Give us it.

The dealer looks at him the way he's seen people look many times, simultaneously pitying and contemptuous, then backs out the lavatory and disappears into the crowd.

The girls have moved to a table and turn away when they see him. They know the change. They've seen it too many times.

He faces the bar and there's a roar of laughter. From the table behind him, where the girls and the other guys are sitting, there's a swell of laughter and he doesn't know, can't be certain but something tells him they're laughing at him.

Is that your champagne? he asks one of the guys, who does his best to ignore him, who looks away and tries to resume his conversation.

I asked you a fucken question, he says, standing above them at the table. I don't think it is your champagne. I don't think you bought that. I think I bought that and I think you're drinking my fucken drink without asking and I think you should fuck off out of it before I take the bottle and crash it over your fucken big heid.

And they look at each other, the women and the men. No one breaks the silence that is suddenly louder than the music and other conversations. They stare at each other, stand up and move away and he takes the arm of one of the women he's had his eye on, the one with the shoulder length dark hair and the big eyes, the one with the nice smile, who brushed her tits against him when she squeezed past on her way to the lavatory.

Where are you going? he says. You're with me.

And he knows it's wrong.

Sorry, he says. Sorry. I'm really really sorry. I lost it. Just for a moment there, I lost it and I'm sorry. Can I talk with you? What's your name again? Tamsin? Is it Tamsin? Is your name Tamsin? Nice name. We're a Jock Tamsin's bairns, eh? Listen. Can I talk with you? Please.

And she turns away, doesn't say anything, turns away and walks to the lavatory.

He follows her.

Look. I know this is out of order. Right. I know this is well out of order and I'm sorry. I'm sorry. I'm really sorry. But I like you, I like you and I want to spend some time with you. Will you talk to me? Please. Say something. Please.

He's standing outside the cubicle door, pleading when the bouncers come in.

I'm sorry, sir. We're going to have to ask you to leave.

What kind of fucken phrase is that: going to have to ask you to leave. That doesnae sound like a phrase anybody who knows anything about the English language would use. That sounds like a phrase an idiot would use. And take your fucken hands off me.

They rip his suit. They rip the top pocket of his suit and while he's yelling that he's going to sue them because the suit cost more than they earn in a fucken year, they march him through the club and out the door, throw him onto the street and go back inside. They close the door and phone the police, while he's out there yelling, telling anybody who'd listen he's going to be with his friends, the real people.

He's staggering. He didn't want this to happen and all he needs is a wee rest to steady himself, so he gets a taxi and slumps in the back and the driver starts talking about golf, how he hasn't been out for a week or two but maybe he'll get out on Sunday if the weather keeps up. Sunday's his day off.

Shut the fuck up, he says. Who gives a fuck about golf?

Who wants to talk about golf except a daft bastard like you. Golf isnae a subject. There is no conversation to be had about golf, especially if one of the participants doesnae play fucken golf. And that's me. So shut the fuck up about bastardin golf.

There's a boundary charge, the driver says.

And that was that till they pulled into the scheme. Sweeties, papers and crisp bags; it's raining, dark and deserted, no street lights, pink curtains tied with a pin or a couple of pins and the bare light bulb showing through the fabric. There's the noise of television and a sing song. Somebody's got a karaoke machine. And the driver's a bit leerie, hoping no one wants a taxi.

Thirty quid, he says.

And he makes a show of producing a wad that would choke a horse, peeling three tens and looking into the driver's mirror.

Imbecile, he says. If you'd asked for fifty you'd've got it.

He puts the money on the back seat and leaves the taxi doors open; the driver has to get out his cab, run round, collect the money, shut the doors and bolt the course.

And as soon as he's away, as soon as the taxi sound fades and he's lit a fag, he's forgotten how he got there, that there ever was a taxi, because it's looking good; in fact, it's looking wonderful.

No one knew, right. Sometimes, not just times like this but other times as well, sometimes he just gets these ideas that are absolutely unbelievable. And this was one of them. He thought, right, when he got thrown out that dump when he left these ungrateful bitches back in that place, he thought, Where can I go? And this idea came into his head. Janice. One word, two syllables, Jah-niss. And he thought he might be able to remember where she stayed. And not only did he remember, but when he arrived, Janice is having a party. The karaoke sound is coming from Janice's place, two storeys up.

He does the stairs two at a time. He knows the door will be open and in he goes, gets a can of beer from the kitchen and there's a woman singing:

Just like a flower,
I'm growing wild.

And Janice sees him. He raises his can and she comes over and the woman's still singing and she asks, How's it goin?

Not too bad. How about yourself?

What've you been up to then?

You know. The usual. Bit of this and a bit of that.

They tell me you're married.

Was.

No more?

Selling the house, everything gone.

Interesting.

And he thinks she's looking at the can. I brought it, he says. I left the rest in the kitchen.

But she's looking at his suit. What happened to you? says Janice in her wee black dress. The top pocket's ripped.

He shrugs: Damsel in distress.

Lucky lady.

He lights two fags and gives her one and she takes a draw and blows smoke in his face and he moves across when she moves away because she's just realised the singing's stopped and everybody's at the window and it's quiet and there's a voice shouting her name, a voice from outside the house is shouting.

Janice. Come to the windae. Come tae the windae, Janice. Janice. Come tae the fucken windae.

And everybody's laughing and staring across the road where this guy on the verandah opposite has a woman bent over, one arm on the wall and the other on the railing and he's at her back hauling her up and down, shouting: I tellt ye. I tellt ye I could dae it, Janice. I'm shagging your pal, Janice. I'm shagging Wee Wilma. You there, Janice?

And Wee Wilma's shouting: It wisnae me, Janice. Honest tae God, hen, it wisnae me. It's him, Janice. He's a dirty pig. It was him that wanted it. It wisnae me. It's him. He's aye on to me. It's his fault.

And by the time the lavvy'd burst and the cistern was running and the lights had gone out and the door was lying open and the booze was done and Janice is on the couch with the mascara running down her face and the lipstick's all over her mouth, he's still there, still hanging about and he'd've stayed, but she said, You'd better go, Right. You'd better go. He'll be back and he'll do his nut if he finds you here. He'll go mental. He'll wreck the place. Honest. You'd better go. I'll be fine. It's nothing. Okay. It's nothing. We'll get the wean her trainers and that'll be that. It's nothing. The wean wanted new trainers and he'd nae money. It isnae serious.

It's raining.

And he's walking into town, trying to thumb a lift.

He doesn't know what happened to the raincoat, he's only got the suit and he's soaked and his new shoes hurt, are letting in and his collar's turned up. And it's starting to bite. He's beginning to see things and he knows what'll happen, he knows what's next and he'll do anything, anything, he'll do anything to stop that and it isn't fair. This is not the time to stop.

Look at it this way. He got the money and fixed himself up with some gear, squared up his mother, which he didn't have to do, she'd never asked for a penny. Then he went for a drink and all was going well till these bastards moved in and got him thrown out and he went to Janice to help her out because he hadn't seen her for a while and Janice was a good sort, an old pal, sure there might have been a bit of something now and again but Janice was a pal. Anyway, he left because he didn't want to cause her any bother and now he's got the shakes, or he's nearly got the shakes, Christsake, what chance have you got with luck like that. He can tell the difference between the shakes and the cold, and this is the shakes. And he's just started. Dear God, what did he get, a couple of hours, three, four hours at the most. And now he's got to carry on. Now he's got to keep drinking to hold off the shakes. And by the time he reaches town, having sat upstairs on a freezing bus, the rain's stopped, so he does the lanes.

He prowls the lanes between Blythswood Square and Argyle Street looking for glasses with drink in them. You know the way youngsters think it's fun to leave the pub and take their glasses with them, walk round with their drinks and when they go up the lane for a pish they've still got the glasses. Sometimes they pish in the glasses and sometimes they don't. You can usually tell the glasses that've been pished in because there's a puddle around them, but you can't tell when it's raining, so he has to smell the glasses.

The lanes are on a hill and he's knackered going from one back door to another, looking for a drink that hasn't been pished in and God knows what time it is, maybe three or four in the morning but it could be one or two, he doesn't know, because his watch has gone, but he's tired and that's good; if he can get a sleep he'll waken with the shakes right enough, but he'll avoid seeing things and if he's got the shakes he can usually get enough by begging, he's done it before and he can do it again, folk think he's ill and always give him something because he sounds all right. So, one way or another, he can start to taper down.

But he's got money, so there's no need to beg. He can turn up at what his mother still calls a licensed grocer and get a drink, even on a Sunday; if they see the state you're in, you'll get it, you'll have to pay twice the price, but you'll still get it. Then he can go home and try to get back to normal. Except this is normal.

For you don't always taper down when you think you'll taper down, you can't come off it when you'd like to come off it because you're not in charge, and what you want has got nothing to do with it; but a sleep's good and you've got to take it when you can get it, so he coories in a doorway and gets the head down for maybe twenty minutes, no more than half an hour, when he hears singing, guys, four or five of them coming up the lane.

Oh-ho auld yin.

Hey, listen, Jakieman, how's it goin?

Anythin tae drink?

What's in there Auldguy? You got a bird in there?

Oh-ho, the auld Jackieman's getting his nookie.

Quite right. Intae it.

He turns and tries to tell them. He turns and gets himself to his knees, then puts his hands on the wall and tries to stand. I'm no a jakie, he says.

If you're no a jakie, how come you're here?

You smell like a jakie.

Look at the state you're in.

Fucken Jakieman.

Tell you what, he says. Tell you what. Listen. Tell you what. I can prove it. Right.

Prove what?

I can prove I'm no a jakie. I've got money. Look. I've got money.

And he holds some notes out at them.

There you are. What'd I tell you. Jakies don't have money, do they? Take it. Eh? Take it. Take the cash and leave us. Okay.

One takes some money.

Then another. And as the third takes the rest, they walk up the lane. He turns away, looking to see how much is left, when one of them runs downhill, leaps into the air, legs out and kicks him on the back.

He doesn't remember much else, except there's a strange sound like someone singing high in the air, like a whisper, something he was struggling to hear as they're kicking him and he's on the cobbles huddled in a ball, muttering, I'm no a jakie. I'm no a jakie. I'm no a jakie.

They go through his pockets and take what's left. One takes his shoes and throws them away. Another takes his tie. Then they piss on him.

He lies there till there's no other sound, till the singing in his head has stopped, and he half walks, stumbles onto the main road where he sits crying in a doorway till the Manna van picks him up.

Regular as the moon, the Manna From Heaven crew have to move premises, maybe three or four times a year, because they don't pay rent. Whatever they get goes on food, clothes, blankets and the like for the guys in the shelter. So they occupy near-derelict buildings and do what they can, volunteers mostly, many recovering or trying to recover, doing this to stay stopped.

A man in a bunnet at the foot of the steps asks if he fancies something to eat, maybe a bowl of soup or a cup of tea.

I'm no a jakie, he says, crying. I'm no a jakie.

Of course not, the wee man says, climbing the steps to sit beside him. I don't mean to be cheeky and I hope you don't think I'm being nosey, but do you have anywhere to stay? We can fix you up with something. It's dry, the beds are comfortable and you'll get fed. You're in an awful mess. It's a good-looking suit. Did you fall? What happened to your shoes?

The van ride's rough. There's a smell from the other guys who look defeated. One is cut and bleeding down the side of his face. The other two scratch themselves. One has open sores.

No one speaks till they're inside the shelter, where there's a crowd round the soup pot and there's trays of leftover sandwiches still in their cellophane wrappers, cakes and scones with jam and margarine and women clean and bandage sores, a chiropodist, a doctor, a nurse and what could be a chemist over by the wall, where there's a rail of clothes and one or two are arguing about a jacket or a jumper. When someone offers him clothes, he refuses: No thank you, he says in a way that lets them know he doesn't take charity.

You'll need a pair of shoes, a woman says. See if these fit.

She likes him. He can tell. She fancies him.

I'll get you socks, she says. And she smiles up at him.

She helps him on with the shoes and socks and he stands and walks around and they fit nicely, better than the last pair.

Thanks, he says to the woman and as he reaches out to touch her face she pulls away.

When that happens, he thinks he's in the wrong place. Someone has made a dreadful mistake. Surely they can tell he shouldn't be here. No harm to the people who are here, good luck to them, but surely they can see the situation he's in is temporary and resolvable. Not that they're at fault. They see down and outs all the time and must get used to treating everyone the same, maybe they can't discriminate, maybe some of the punters, who are probably called clients, will complain if anyone is treated differently, so they have to treat everyone the same.

And then a fresh idea arrives and sometimes he wonders where those ideas come from because when they arrive they are so complete. Borrow. That's the word. That's what he has to do. Borrow. It isn't stealing, it isn't begging and it isn't really a loan; it's like a loan, except it's temporary. He'll pay it back when the house is sold, sure as God, he'll do it.

And while he's thinking this out, he leaves the church; there's no point staying because he'd never get a sleep and he doesn't want anything to eat and he shouldn't be there anyway, he could get fleas, lice, anything. A can of lager would go down well, so it's best to leave them to it.

There's a stretch of vacant ground beside the church, the street's intact, but the tenements have gone, with a bonfire near the middle, burned out cars and lorries. There's puddles and boxes, piles of stones, rubbish and folk all over the place, groups and knots of people talking and drinking and smoking and trying to keep warm. He wanders through it all, remembering something he'd never known. These people were his people, the real people, with neither sham nor pretence, entirely free of responsibilities, no children, wives or gaffers, only friends. Their responsibility was to themselves and each other. They were the gentlemen who roamed the countryside, stopping where they fancied, getting a cup of tea and a bite to eat at the big farmhouse kitchens, taking a day's work here or there, helping with the harvest, digging drains, logging and felling, repairing fences, building dykes.

And maybe there would be singing in the bothy and someone might have a melodeon or a mouth organ, maybe a fiddle, or maybe all three and there'd be whisky, of course, and a drop or two of beer, nothing much, just enough to put you right, enough to give you a glow. And there might be a woman around the place; maybe the farmer had a daughter and she'd take a shine to him.

Summer days would bring them closer. Small intimacies would pass between them, smiles and glances, the occasional touch; nothing much, just the way her hand would linger over his, or she would smile when he spoke, how she was always pleased to see him. And the other men would notice and ask when he was getting his feet under the kitchen table. The farmer would know, though he'd pretend not to, but his wife would know and when the men were sitting down to their food in the long kitchen table, she'd give him an extra drop of soup and a slice or two of bread and she'd always make a fresh pot of tea when he was around with something newly baked, a scone or a pancake with butter and homemade jam.

And maybe he'd shelter her from the rain. They'd be caught in a storm or a sudden squall on the hill and they'd run for shelter and arrive breathless by a copse of trees where he'd take off his jacket and she'd look up to him and smile as he put the jacket over her shoulders which would make him bold enough to put his arm round her waist when he moved her through the door in front of him going into the house.

And this was maybe where he'd kiss her, or she'd kiss him, when she'd want to know of his life before they met. He'd tell her how he longed to settle, how he'd taken to the road because of difficulties he had never even mentioned because no one understood; how people told him to pull himself together, but no one knew how he felt, not even his mother; how his father was a remote authoritarian who came home from work, watched television and died; how the family scattered and no one stayed in touch; how he never felt good enough; how he never felt he belonged anywhere, never felt a part of things; how he always seemed to be on the outside looking in; how he always, more than anything, he always felt vulnerable, except when he drank and when he stopped drinking, the pain began. People said he should stop drinking and feel better. But when he stopped he felt worse. And his whole life had been a struggle to resolve these things and when he could not resolve them he felt a failure because that was what everyone said he was. But he had his dreams, he knew he could succeed if someone would try to understand him, try to listen, accept him for what he was rather than try to mould him into what they wanted him to be. And for the first time he felt he'd met someone who not only understood, but who could change things, make it better. And she'd lean across, squeeze his hand and kiss him.

And with the harvest home, the farmer would ask if he'd plans for the winter. They could do with a man around the place and if he fancied staying he could see to the painting and repairs that were needing done, then he'd be glad to have him. He could think about it. Take his time. No need to rush. The harvest was in, there was the dance coming up and he could tell him then.

She looked wonderful; especially when she asked if he was going to the dance and if he was looking forward to it and maybe they could have a dance together and he'd smile and say, We'll see, and she smiled back. And she'd got a new frock and her hair was up and shining and she'd be wearing lipstick, sitting by her mother when he walked across the floor and asked if she'd do the Pride of Erin Waltz. And she came closer when he put his arm round her waist and it was as if they'd been dancing together for years and he asked if she'd stay up and she said okay, but the next dance was an Eightsome Reel and when she set to him and turned him she looked straight into his face and he did the same when he set to her and he said, maybe she'd like to have a drink and she said she was fine, but she'd take a glass of lemonade. And while he fetched it, her mother smiled at her and other men came over to ask her to dance and she said, No thank you. And he brought her the lemonade, with a beer, an ordinary pale ale for himself and they sat together, drinking and she said she knew her Dad had mentioned staying on and she hoped he would. And they got on the floor for a Lomond Waltz and he said he'd stay if she wanted him to, and she squeezed his hand and they were together, sometimes dancing, sometimes sitting and talking, till the end of the night.

He'd hold her hand going home and from then it was inevitable. They'd celebrate New Year with their engagement and marry the following year, combining their wedding with the harvest dance. And their wedding would be wonderful, children running round, the boys in kilts, girls in party frocks, a barrel of beer and lots of whisky, with a buffet of quiches and salad stuff, chicken, salmon and lots of dancing to the fiddle and accordion. The dances would be interrupted by songs and while someone was singing one of the older men would take him round the back where his new father-in-law and two or three of the men were laughing.

O, you'll need this the night, someone would say, offering a bottle with a Bell's yellow label, though the whisky wasn't Bell's, but was, he supposed, illegal stuff, made from a still at the top of the glen, the stuff that circulated around the New Year and was always produced on family occasions.

And when the sandwiches had gone and the last few children were crying, when the dancing was about to start again, when the red-faced men in shirts and braces were talking a bit too loudly and some of the women were giggling, she would look at him, changed now into her new dress, and ask if it was time to leave.

And so their life together would begin. In time there would be children and they would grow old together, with the farm passing from one generation to the other. There would be others like him, men who came to the door and were never turned away. No matter the conditions, they knew they'd always get a welcome, a bowl of soup and a slice of bread at his door. For he'd never disguised the fact that he'd been one of them, which, he felt, gave hope to other men of the road, especially those who were lost, out of their depth.

His spirit was free and his heart was as open to the wonders of discovery as their hearts and minds and souls had been, but they were constrained. They rebelled, refused to conform, refused to be pigeonholed into drab existence. They were the true political activists, humanity's passive resisters, those who said, No, then got up and left. Theirs was a non-conformist, rebel heart. He loved them, loved the idea of them and would always be one of them, even though he was also the farmer. He would treat them well, see they were well paid, rather than exploited.

But there was the favourite bit, when he and his wife were not yet married, in the springtime, after their engagement when they were discussing their future, when she would take him for a stroll through her father's woods, maybe up by the bit where they'd sheltered from the rain and she'd remind him and he'd smile and she'd say that was when she fell in love and then she'd apologise for interrupting him, for he'd be telling her how he'd like to give these folk work and she'd say that was how she'd always felt and he was surprised and not really surprised, more delighted that this was another aspect of their love, that they felt and thought the same way, that no one had to sacrifice a principle or pretend to be different and they'd look at each other and she'd reach up and kiss him and he'd put his arms around her and she'd fall to the ground with him on top of her and he'd be gentle with her, but she doesn't mind because she wants him so much and tells him no man has ever made her feel this way, that she never so much as imagined a man, any man, could make her feel this way, and she guides him into her and as he gently makes his way up inside, her cries echo through the forest, frightening a flock of pigeons who take off to rise above the trees and circle the sky.

Someone threw a chair on the fire. It flared into sudden flame, with sparks and smoke swirling upwards.

Excuse me, sir.

A man whose voice was hard to understand was standing beside him. He had sunken eyes, big hands and a tattooed neck.

You look like an educated man. Perhaps you can settle a dispute, well, a discussion really, a point of disputation. My friends and I were wondering who was the greatest painter? Van Gogh or Rembrandt? There has to be an answer? So, Van Gogh or Rembrandt, who's it to be?

Do you know?

I have my opinion.

But you don't know?

Well, I think I know.

Then, you tell me.

I asked the question to find your opinion.

Why?

Because, I thought you'd have an opinion.

I don't.

Not at all?

Not at all.

That's hard to believe. Who's the greatest painter, Van Gogh or Rembrandt, and you don't have an opinion?

Van Gogh.

Sorry?

Van Gogh.

I don't think so.

Okay, it was Rembrandt.

Why?

Why what?

Why did you say it was Van Gogh and then change your mind?

Because I thought better of it.

Not because you ceased to believe Van Gogh was the better painter?

How many? asked a man who had joined them. He'd been listening to the conversation while trying to roll a fag, a man with a sports jacket and a red scarf, whose hair looked as though it had been frizzed and pulled back across his head.

Sorry, he said, when he realised he had their attention. Sorry. One thing and one thing only. Right. How many men does it take to make a quorum? There y'are now, tell me that? Yese canny tell me cause yese don't know.

Six.

Naw.

Five.

Naw.

Nine.

Yese'll never get it.

An I've another one. What can you no multiply?

The number of men it takes to make a quorum.

Naw.

Yes. Yes. Definitely yes.

Naw.

We don't know the number of men it takes to make a quorum, and since you can't multiply what you don't know we can't multiply the number of men it takes to make a quorum. Which was what you asked.

Infinity.

Same thing.

Ye canny multiply infinity. Listen, Big Man. A favour. Right. A silly wee favour. Hear me out now. D'ye fancy sellin the *Big Issue*?

What?

Know how they mark them through the sheets; well, I got some that havenae been marked and we can do a wee deal.

I think you've got the wrong person.

Nae offence. I didnae mean to offend you.

I'm not a *Big Issue* seller.

Sammy was scoofing for scrap and Charlie was singing,

trying to remember the words of a song he'd written. Boxy was standing at the edge of the fire. When the wind changed he was covered in smoke, but he didn't move. He just stood there in his black, ankle tapper coat, staring straight ahead.

Hey, he shouted to no one.

The smoke covered him again.

Where is he? he asked when he emerged. The guy that was here, where is he?

Who?

Him that was here.

The smoke covered him and when it cleared he didn't speak.

Charlie remembered some of the words:

Thingme, thingme, dah dah rah dah,
Thingme baby, I love you.

Then Annie started dancing. She turned round twice and fell in the fire.

Is this any use? Sammy shouted. He held a bit of rusted machinery above his head. It had a wheel and a handle and was screwed to a block of wood. One side was painted green and peeling.

Anybody know what this is? It's good gear this. Anybody know?

Ya bastard, Annie shouted, when she burned her hands trying to get up. Somebody help me up. Quick. Get me up.

Moose Robert tried to help, but Annie pulled him forward and he stumbled into the smoke.

Watch yourself in that smoke, said Boxy.

Annie's coat was smouldering and her boots were melting.

Yous're bastards, she shouted. Bastards.

Charlie was singing and Boxy never moved. Someone pulled Annie out of the fire.

Don't fling my thing on the fire, Sammy said. That's good gear. There's a few quid in that.

I need to go to the hospital, Annie said.

Oh-ho. A shout came from the other side of the fire. Then, from nowhere came a man on a bike with four others chasing. At first he was wobbly, for the bike was old with twisted wheels and flat tyres, but he soon balanced himself and went round the dump shouting for folk to get out the way, with the others chasing, barking for a shot on the bike. He collapsed near a crowd of men sitting in a huddle on the other side of the fire and as the group dispersed one man stood out from the others.

He was dressed in a white raincoat and was wearing a tie. His shoes were polished. He approached the men in twos or threes and could have been a preacher looking for someone to come to their church, or maybe to pray with him. It was common to see groups of down and outs and prostitutes singing hymns and praying beside a van that gave them clean clothes and food. A sign on the side of the van said Jesus Loves Down & Outs & Prostitutes.

Libby, the man said. I'm looking for Libby.

We don't know any Libby.

She's young, early twenties. Blonde.

Could be anybody. Wha'd ye want her for?

I need to see her. I lost my money.

Wha'sat got tae dae wi Libby?

Nothing, really. I don't care about the money. I need my card. She can keep the money. It's the card. I need the card, for where I work.

Where'd ye work?

This was a fat guy with a crew cut and an Adidas T-shirt that didn't cover his belly. His jacket was too tight. He was smoking with one eye closed, reminiscent of a night watchman who let Derek sleep in his hut. Ages ago, this was, when he was young, maybe 18 or 19, when he was coming back from some party or other and had to walk home because there were no buses and he landed up in the watchman's hut. The watchman took out his glass eye and anytime Derek looked all he could see was the red blob where an eye should have been.

Have you ever been with a man? he asked. Men are better. Most folk want girls, but what do they know? Young lassies know nothing. They think they're doing you a favour being seen with them, never mind letting you touch them. A man's better. You get a better thrill off a man.

In an office, I work in an office. Down by the river. It's a big building with tight security because it's the government, Ministry of Defence actually. Not that I've got anything to do with real defence, but if I lose my pass there'll be a security check and that'll mean I'll have to tell them.

Tell them what?

About Libby.

What about her?

My wife died about six or seven months ago and it's been unbearable. I don't know what made me do it. I'd gone through town often, late at night even, just going through town on my way home and I'd seen these girls and it never crossed my mind. Then, one night.

What's this got t'dae wi Libby?

Two nights ago we went to a hotel, well, a bed and breakfast place in Renfrew Street, up by the Art School. She took my wallet. I didn't know.

How'd ye know it was her?

When we got into the room, I had the wallet when I paid her. And it wasn't there in the morning. She'd gone when I wakened. It was awful. She'd gone and she'd taken the card. It was in the wallet. And I told them. I had to tell them I'd left it at home. I said it was in my other jacket. And they'll expect me to turn up with it. The money's not important. She can keep the money. I'll give her more if she needs it. I came to see her, to ask for the card, to find out what happened. I mean, supposing, just supposing she threw the wallet away and the card was in the wallet, that would be awful, the worst possible thing to have happened. It could cost me my job. I asked in town and they told me she'd be here. But, I think I've made a mistake.

A crowd had gathered and he knew he was in trouble. He'd said too much. He thought he was being reasonable and if he was reasonable with them they'd be reasonable with him, if he explained his position they would understand. Now he knew he was wrong. He should have told them he was looking for Libby because he fancied her, because he'd been with her once and fancied it again. Anything. He should have told them anything other than what he'd told them. His back was to the fire. He stared at them, swallowing hard, his eyes glistening.

Give us the money an we'll see Libby gets it.

But I need the card. I came to see Libby.

And you've brought her money?

I haven't got money. I can get money, but not tonight.

A stone hit him above the eye. He stepped back into the fire and fell. His coat was burning and he ripped it off, trying at the same time to stand. He fell again into the ashes and with his coat blazing near him and blood running down his face, he tried to escape. They were laughing. They pushed him from one to the other and back. Every once in a while as he bounced from one to the other, someone would take a swipe, lash out and hit him across the face, or land a punch which would make him scream or double with pain, then someone hauled him upright and spun him off in another direction, until, weeping, his face bruised and swollen, he was shoved into the fire.

The fat crew cut and Adidas T-shirt man held out his hand. And the man who was looking for Libby handed him some notes.

That it?

He nodded his head.

I don't believe you.

He shook his head and started breathing quickly, sobbing, with tears running down his cheeks. Steam rose from the hot ash where he had pished himself.

The big guy stepped aside and the man staggered past the guys with the bike and round the back of the fire, dazed and wandering, looking for an escape, gradually making his way onto the road where he was nearly knocked over by a car coming into the field. A girl got out the car, then shouted back at the driver: Wait, darlin. Right. Wait. Wait. Okay. Wait.

And she ran towards the group at the fire, in her short skirt and boots, her face unwashed and painted, her hair uncombed, her handbag round her shoulder, she ran towards the group at the fire and shouted, Eddie. Eddie. Eddie. Gie's a score deal. She was holding a twenty pound note in her hand.

Run, said the man whose coat was smouldering by the fire. Run, he said to the driver. Get out of here.

And the car turned round. It ran over the bike and when they started shouting the crowd by the fire looked up.

And the girl ran towards the car, then turned to give the Adidas man the money, shouting for the car to stop. And Derek, who had been watching, detached and uninvolved, ran after the car. He arrived in time to see the sobbing man shouting for the car to stop as it revved down the street and turned out of sight and behind them both, from the fire in the field the girl is shouting, FuckFuckFuckenBastards; how the fuckenbastards; how the fuck am I gonnae get back intae toon?

Nothing changes and everything is repeated, constantly another the same. You open a door to leave and are back where you started.

He wakens in Alan's place.

This time, it's bad. His heart is slamming against his chest and he can't see properly. He presses his eyes shut, but it's still fuzzy, as if he's looking through a rain-soaked window or trying to find a mountain in the mist.

So he rolls off the couch onto the floor, trying to find a place to be comfortably ill, where he can stretch and let himself hurt, but he's no sooner on the floor than he tries to rise back onto the couch.

Now he is hyperventilating, in turns crying and yelling. He knows what he needs.

He turns the sofa upside down, strips the bed and empties the kitchen cupboards, knowing there would be no booze unless he put it there, but hoping he might find something.

He turns on the radio, loud, frantic music to drive him harder, hauling bottles and boxes onto the floor, clearing the fridge and cupboards. He sits in the middle of the mess trailing his hands through the eggs and flour and sugar and oil and rubbing it into his body.

Don't worry, he says to no one. This is fine. All you have to do is get a drink and then you can come back and clear this place up. And a wash. Get yourself washed.

He speaks these instructions to himself, trying to shave and failing, running out of energy when it comes to changing his shirt. The bath defeats him. He closes the door with the music blaring.

I have to clear this place. I'll come back and fix this, he says on his way downstairs. Alan can't come back and find the place like this. I'll have to fix it.

He got off the bus slowly, holding onto the railing as he lowered his feet and running across the pavement to grip the fence. He gathered himself and, slowly at first, walked up the road, his jacket collar turned as if against the chill, scanning to see if anyone knew he was there.

He was shaking. And every now and then he stopped as if trying to brush off a fly, hitting the air with his hand, like a boxer. It's nothing. He sees something that isn't there.

He had no money and no way of getting money and had tried to get booze on tick, but he knew that was a non-starter, so he left the shop and got a bus to his mother's because he needed a drink and if she knew the state he was in she'd give it to him, she'd look after him, but he didn't want her to see him this way, couldn't stand it when she looked at him and didn't say anything, but she didn't need to say anything because he knew what she was thinking.

And it was a loan. He was borrowing the money. He wasn't stealing. If she knew how much he needed it she'd give it to him. He'd pay her back. Hand on heart, on his life and hers. As soon as he was on his feet, as soon as he was back to normal, he'd give her the money. He'd done it not that long ago. How much had he given her? Hundreds. And she'd been pleased. She was pleased to see him doing well. So she knew it was safe. She knew it was a loan. He'd get a drink, square himself up and fix things.

And he knew. He knew how important this insurance money was to her, money she'd set aside to pay for her funeral; money she said should never be spent. But it wouldn't be spent. Not all of it. He wouldn't take it all. He'd take some, enough to get by.

He walked past the house. There was no light in the sitting room, which usually meant she wasn't in. And her neighbours weren't in. How much was this house worth now, these solid bungalows with cars in the drive and an alarm facing the street.

He walked up the lane, climbed a fence that was three doors up from his mother's, he couldn't remember the woman's name, but she was a Christian who had taken him to church and asked him to get baptised.

He was exhausted when he reached his mother's window, wondering how to get in. He checked if the windows were snibbed, or if the back door was on the latch. Everything was shut. He thought he might wait till she got in, then wondered how she'd react, seeing him in this condition. Anyway, he didn't know where she was; she could be hours away. Anything could happen. He needed the money.

He smashed the window and cut his hands sweeping the glass or trying to reach round to open the window. Somewhere behind him a bird sang. There was no other sound. He couldn't hear the alarm. Thank God, she'd forgotten. He crawled through the window, ripping his shirt and trousers, hauled himself through, fell onto the kitchen floor and with blood dripping from his arm ran upstairs and ransacked her bedroom, opening drawers and slinging clothes, papers and photographs, looking for the dark green book and the brown envelope with the money folded and counted with the slip of paper saying how much she'd saved. She had it and he knew she had it because she'd told him. She showed him and told him this was what she wanted.

In Lambhill, she said, beside your dad.

He went downstairs, through the living room and into the kitchen, then he ran upstairs, lifted the bed and pulled off the covers, tried to see what was under the bed and went back to the dresser but the drawers were opened and their contents scattered and he battered his head off the wall, shouting, just yelling, battering his head off the wall and yelling and when he turned to go back downstairs, the envelope was on the floor. It must have been in the first drawer he opened.

He ran up the hill to the Morvern. This was the hard bit. What to get.

He didn't want to go too soon, so he'd better get beer. But he needed something strong to stop the shakes and the wee bits and pieces that came to the corner of his eyes. He didn't want to get that awful way, when he knew what was happening but could do nothing about it, or that he blacked out altogether, or worse still went into a blackout when he was behaving normally, but could remember nothing later. What he needed was something to steady him, to calm him down.

He'd get beer and if that didn't work he'd get some stronger stuff and if that didn't work, he'd have to get whisky or vodka. Not whisky. Look what happened last time he had whisky. Vodka was better. He didn't want to get anything. He hated this, wanting to stop and scared to stop. Getting better meant doing what he didn't want to do, doing what he thought was nonsense, what he didn't think would work. And drinking was pretty much the same. But this time would be different. He'd learned his lesson. This time he'd stop before it got too bad. He knew. He knew when it was getting bad and this time he'd stop.

He bought four cans of super lager and a halfbottle of vodka for the bus.

The bastards at the wine bar wouldn't let him in and Janice's boyfriend was back and he saw Jenni. He was sure it was her in the wine bar. She was going to come over but he was talking to Wee Wilma and she didn't want to embarrass him.

Apart from Jenni, it's not quite clear, for he goes in and out of what he remembers and he doesn't know because this time it isn't working the way it worked before. He had it all worked out. He thought he would drink till he had to get sober and stay sober till he had to get drunk. But this was different and not entirely unknown. There had been times when he knew he couldn't stop, times when memory was a bit of land in the dark and the sweep of a lighthouse lamp comes round and he can see things for a wee while, then it goes dark again, really dark, then it gets a wee bit lighter and just as his eyes are adjusting the lamp comes round and on it goes, all the time so he doesn't know what's real and what's not right, that maybe things he thought had happened, didn't happen.

He remembered bringing a tray of drinks from the bar to where a lassie and her parents are sitting, skinny with chipped nail varnish and lipstick on her teeth. She'd told him her sister was babysitting with her boyfriend so they could get the place to themselves and she was out with her Ma and Da for a drink.

He puts the drinks on the table and sits down beside her and there's someone singing and no one's looking so he feels her leg under the table. She pushes his hand away and tells him to stop, but smiles as though she doesn't want him to stop, but tells him to stop and smiles as if to say she's embarrassed with him doing this in front of her Ma and Da even though everybody's steaming and there's a woman at the microphone singing 'I Will Survive' and she looks at him as if to say, Later. We can do this later. We'll get a carry-out and say we're going to the same party as Ma and Da and give them something so they'll be all right and then go up to the house and chase the sister and her daft boyfriend and then she screams.

A louse is crawling down his neck.

What? he says. What's up?

Fucksake, her Da says, Fucksake man, you're boggin.

And the lassie sits round beside her Ma and takes her Ma's hand and the barman says, Right. Come on. Get you to fuck out of here afore we need to fumigate the place.

And that's when he's sure he saw her, definitely saw her, when he's in the wine bar in his new suit, looking good and she smiled and came over.

Well, well, well, she said. Look who's here and looking good.

And on the way back home she's kissing his neck in the taxi with his hand inside her thigh, stroking, and she's whispering, You, only you, as he stretches her across the bed with her dress open and round her waist and he's inside her.

No fucking around?

No fucking around.

Me?

You. Only you. And you're going to stop.

Absolutely. I'm done with all that.

Then he's back in town, drinking cans and walking, singing to himself every now and then just singing, till they tell him to fucken shut up and move on and the lassies on the corners tell him to get to fuck before he gets lifted and this woman who looked as if she'd had too many children with a wee skirt, a red coat, smudged lipstick and what looks like a wig asks if he fancies a drink and when he goes to take it, she turns away, then says, All right. And he gives her a drink out his can and they get a taxi and she takes some money and comes back with a carry-out of wine and beer and there's enough for a couple of lines and a smoke and she starts chopping the stuff up in the taxi, shouting at the driver to watch when he turns the bends and he's rolling a monster joint and they manage to get a couple of lines and she drinks a can of beer in one go and gets out the taxi at a block of flats where at whatever time it is two or three in the morning, there's kids on bikes and guys in shell suits and a group of two or three lassies shout at her, one of them turning to yell into the darkness, Anne Marie, that's your mammy hame, and Anne Marie tells the guy to hurry up as they hold on to each other, a can each and him with the joint and they get into the lift where the smell hits him as soon as the door opens and she kisses him and says, Hold on, right, just hold on, and the next thing he hears is her having a pish and the doors open and a guy and his dog are standing there, he's got the joint and the can and she's having a pish when the doors open and the guy in his combat gear and boots with the big Rottweiler's standing there and she shouts at him, Shut the fucken door, pervert, and they get into her flat which has no name on the door and is lying open because somebody's broken in and the place hasn't been repaired and there's nothing, no linoleum, cooker, nothing, but a single room with an unmade bed and clothes across the floor and there's no electricity, but standing at the window by the city lights she shows him her collection of two or three furry animals and hunts around, coming back with a couple of candle douts which she lights and then they start drinking the wine by the neck, a bottle each and there's music blaring from the wee tranny and she's doing this strip dance and she dives on him and they roll across the bed and he begins to undress her, and she pushes him away saying she'll do it and he's to watch and she does this strip dance prancing around the place and she takes off her top and her bra and her skirt and while she's taking off her boots some money falls onto the floor, could be anything, but there's definitely a couple of tens and that could be a twenty or a fiver, so there's at least twenty-five quid, he's thinking, and she's doing this dance thing, struggling with the other boot and he stuffs what he can into his pocket, grabs the money and runs and she sees him and goes for him, but he wallops her and goes out the door and heads for the stairs and as he's jumping the stairs two, three at a time he can hear her at the window shouting and he looks out the broken stair window to see what's going on and they're waiting, with sticks and Christknows what, waiting for him to come out the front door, so he has to think fast, no danger, he's got the money and a drink or two and he's fine, just fine, all he has to do is think and then the door crashes open and he can hear them on the stairs and he doesn't know how far up he is, only two or three, so he runs to the next landing and throws himself down the waste chute, into the bins at the bottom in with all the dead food and rubbish and the rats run in all directions when he lands and he jumps to the top of the bin and dives over and still has to come out the high flat's door but there's only two or three and he just barges his way through them and carries on away from the buildings across a big bit of vacant ground with bottles crashing round him and barking dogs chasing him up a hill and onto a field where there's a white light shining and he slips in the mud but carries on, sliding and running across the field into the darkness where someone's singing.

> *Did you not see my lady*
> *Go down the garden singing?*
> *Blackbird and thrush were silent*
> *To hear the alleys ringing.*

No idea, don't know how it happened, but he's back in the lane and he could have been on a late-night bus and the guy wakened him when they got to George Square, or that could have been another time, what is certain about this time is that he's in the lane, back in a doorway and the shakes are on him and he tries to drink a can of beer and he can't, he can't even get it to his lips and he sits there sweating, knowing that if he gets it to his lips and manages to get a drink out of it, he'll be sick, if he's lucky, but he has to get it, has to do something to keep that stuff away and then it's too late, it doesn't matter what he does or doesn't do because this time it hasn't worked, and he looks at his hand and closes his eyes, but it's worse when he does that so he opens his eyes and sees it again, maggots crawling over his hand and he screams and runs and tries to wipe them off his hand but they won't go, because they're multiplying, they're on his hand and his arm and his neck and face and they're all over him, all over his body and no matter what he does they won't go away and he runs and runs and runs and keeps on running out into Renfield Street, out into the middle of the traffic screaming for help, shouting for someone, anyone to help him, the maggots are eating him, gnawing at his insides and they're even in his eyes and he can't see and soon he won't be able to hear, though he knows people are shouting and there's car horns blazing and he reckons he must be in the middle of the road in the middle of the traffic, shouting and screaming when he thinks he can see the blue lights and hear the police or ambulance and he could be in the middle of the traffic but he can't move and he's on the floor and the straps are digging into the small of his back and he keeps trying to sit up, but the effort it takes just to turn leaves him exhausted and he can't sit up, because the straps are holding him down and they're tied, tied round his back and he knows he can't stay there, he can't stay like that or he'll die lying on the floor and he has to sit up and he must have slept for a bit or maybe he passed out because they gave him something, he was sure he felt the needle, so he got something, and he tries again, tries to move himself by the shoulders and this time he's moving, he can feel the floor pressing against him, first down one side, then another, stopping and sleeping and stopping and sleeping, moving one shoulder then another, pressing the floor with his feet and moving his shoulders till his back's to the wall and he isn't off the floor but at least he's sitting and he can feel his hair wet and he knows there's sweat running down his face and this is it this time, never again, definitely, never again, this is it, he means it this time, get me out of this, he says to no one or maybe it's a prayer, perhaps he's praying, making a bargain, please, please, please get me out of this and I'll never drink again and there's the itch, the itch and the sweat and the sweat causes the itch for there's a bead of sweat running down his face from his brow to the top of his nose, sliding down the bridge of his nose and he wants to wipe it, at first he thinks he can just move his arm and wipe it away, but he can't, he wants to wipe it, but can't because his hands are tied, so he tries to shake it free, rattles his head from side to side, but still it's there and the itch is getting worse and it won't move so he tries to wipe it off the wall because it's not only itchy now but painful, it's getting sore and he can't get to it, he can't get his face round far enough so he burns the side of his face against the wall and the sweat and the itch burn into his face and he wants to scream but he can't, he can't scream, because that would be the end, he knows if he screams he'll lose it, lose the lot, but the sweat bead's still running down his nose and it's gathering and there's other bits coming and it's going to drip and he feels the drip and the itch and the sweat running down his nose and he screams and that's it: Shhh, there there there, it's all right now, all right, there we are, that's better isn't it, and that's a woman's voice, he's heard it before but he doesn't know whose voice it is, a friendly voice, a woman's voice, talking as if she is talking to children and the worse thing is not being there, being there's all right because most of the time you don't know you're there, but every once in a while you get a flash and you know that when you get that flash they have to give you something so you don't want the flash you only want the woman's voice saying There there there, it's all right now, Shoosh, but it doesn't always stay that way because every now and then you get a flash, a woman in a nurse's uniform in a white room, and other men in beds, or a procession of men, mostly in dressing gowns and pyjamas, though some are dressed badly, some hold hands, many are quivering and cannot control their saliva. Come along, she says. Come along, there we are now there, there, there, come along, that's good, I hope you're hungry, the voice says to the slow procession of trembling men walking down the long corridor towards the dining room, getting their exercise for the day.

3

I didn't recognise the voice on the phone.

I don't think we've met, he said. My name's Alan Grant.

I don't remember the name.

Derek Anderson used to work for me.

And his wife worked for you?

Jenni, yeah.

I know who you are.

So. How is Derek these days?

Pretty much the same. Derek's in nappies. He's in bed more or less all day, gets spoon-fed and occasionally, if a nurse can find the time she'll hold a cigarette to his mouth so's he can take a draw or two. No one knows for sure, but as far as they can tell he doesn't know what's going on. But that might not be the case. Maybe he does know.

You in touch?

Not really. There's no communication. I go up once or twice a month and sit for a while, half an hour, something like that. I tell him what's going on, but there's no response. It's like being with a dead person.

There but for the grace of God go I.

Something like that.

What else is there for a man like you?

What do you mean?

You stand aside, duty done and move on, accept the weariness and incomprehensibility of God's will and shrug it off as none of your business. Isn't that right?

Not entirely. It isn't as cold, or as detached, as you suggest. And given your role in these events, you're in no position to judge; at least I tried to help. Now, you tell me something: why did you phone here and how did you get my number?

Jenni, for reasons I don't know, but can well imagine, would like to talk to you. She's scared to phone and asked if I'd contact you. She gave me your number. Would you mind if she called?

I don't think it's a good idea.

I'll tell her you've moved on. Goodbye.

Before you do that, something?

Yeah?

How much did you give him?

Eh?

The back money. How much was it? How much did you give him? Enough to kill him, or just enough to get him out the way?

I don't know what you're talking about.

I think you do. I think you know perfectly well what I'm talking about. How long is it since Derek worked for you? And how long does it take to work out how much he was due, if anything. And whose idea was it, yours, or Jennifer's? Who came up with the idea of paying him off with a wad of money at such a convenient time?

I've nothing more to say to you.

You haven't said very much. So, it was your idea?

The line went dead.

Two or three days later, I'd been working late and was walking home when a girl came from a doorway and stood in front of me, forcing me to face her.

I'm not begging, she said. I don't want money. I'm not a beggar.

There was a gust of laughter as three or four boys came out a Chinese restaurant and ran towards the bus stop. Someone was selling the *Daily Record*.

Do you know what epilepsy is? she asked.

I nodded.

I need you to sit with me. Do you mind staying till I feel

better?

She took me into a damp, dark close. We sat on the bottom steps. She stared at the ground, eyes closed and hands on her lap, taking small, shallow breaths, her torso scarcely moving.

I want to go home, she said. I need to go home. It isn't far. You can come with me to the station or all the way home if you like.

Where do you stay?

Motherwell. I need money to get there.

Where do you get the train?

Central. You can give me your address. I'll give you mine. I'll send you the money. Or you can get in touch. I need to go home. I need to get to Motherwell. The last train's at twenty to twelve. I could come home with you.

She stood up. There was a noise from the back.

It's rats, she said, lifting her top. She had what looked like a deep wound on her left side, as though she had been stabbed just below the rib cage, which was showing through. The wound had been plastered. The plaster was dirty and covered in dried blood. A wound on her left arm where her wrists had been slashed was also plastered.

I gave her a fiver and she took two 50 pence pieces from the change in my pocket: For the phone, she said, trembling.

Epileptics don't get into that state.

I've had fits.

I quite believe it. What are you on?

Nothing.

Do you want help?

I want you to hold me, she said.

I could feel the bones through her clothes. She smelled of cigarettes and dried lacquer. Her breath was grim.

Do you want me? she asked. Do you want me as a woman? A woman wants to be wanted.

Let's get you to the station.

She dropped her arms and walked away from me, out the

close and onto the street. She ran across the road and down a flight of stairs to a basement café. She did not look back.

But that night, just before sleep, she stood in front of me again in her dirty red top, jeans that were supported by her hips, her jerkin opened.

There are things in the attic I know nothing about.

With the approach of autumn, as mountains of clouds scud across the sky I open the fanlight, let down the ladder and creak towards a dark and airy, carpeted place where remnants of my previous selves are stacked.

I don't know why I hoard the stuff. I can't explain the attraction of broken furniture, pictures with fractured frames, machines of one sort or another, old systems, things that need mending and never will be fixed. Most of it isn't mine. There's stuff I've inherited and things I've acquired. The pictures are mine, but most of the other stuff's been handed down with bits and pieces I might have gathered, here and there. It's not that I'm sentimental, not about this stuff. It's just that I can't get rid of it, not on my own.

So with the first snows of autumn, when I feel the city is a steppe, when wolves are howling on the stairs and bears pad through the street corner birches, when letters take forever or never come, when I am wasted with boredom and argue over trivia, when I long to be in a place I'll never visit, when life is far away and the samovar is cold, I'll take the coffee, squat on the floor and rummage round.

I was in the attic when she called. The sound of her voice surprised me. She was breathless and nervous, as though she'd worried about phoning, had dialled the number a dozen or more times and replaced the receiver, then, all of a sudden, let it ring. She tried to sound casual, to make nothing of it, but she could barely speak. Her throat was dry. She didn't quite say, Hell, but something like it, Hell, with a gasp, a fall of breath at the end.

I hope you don't mind. You don't mind, do you? You don't mind me phoning? How are you?

I'm fine, really well. How about you?

Still on your own?

Uh-huh.

No one new on the scene?

Not really.

Taking it easy?

Something like that.

Very sensible. It's good to hear your voice again. I've missed it.

You could have phoned.

I wasn't sure.

I wondered how you'd been, what you were doing, that sort of thing. How's London?

There's so much to do. And you've got to keep active, otherwise you just shrivel, don't you. You just go into a wee cocoon and when you're in there it's safe and cosy and you don't want to go out. So you've got to make yourself do things. See people.

Have you made friends?

Here and there.

Tell me about Alan?

I was with Alan, but that didn't work out, so I was lucky enough to land another job. I'd met some people and one of them needed a receptionist. I did some temping, took a word processing course, that sort of thing. I'm doing all right.

Where are you?

I work for a gallery. It can get boring, but it's better than just reception. I talk to the clients, show them round, find out what they want and see if we can provide it. It's good fun.

And you see Alan?

When he's down. The office here is pretty well self-supporting. He's got a few contracts and they're always bidding for things, so he's in London maybe once a month. Not that

I see him every time, but he gives me a call and maybe drops by and we sometimes meet up and have dinner or go to the theatre, something like that, except the London theatres are full of Americans. Every play you go to, you'd think it was New York, just from the accents.

Why did you ask Alan to contact me?

I wanted to speak to you. I was upset. And I wondered how you were.

What did Alan say?

What do you mean?

Did he think it was a good idea?

He said I should let sleeping dogs lie. But it's all very well for him. That's why I left. He was good enough; I mean, he's all right to work for, but there were too many other things going on, know what I mean?

No.

He reminded me of my past. Every time, well not every time, but there were times when I looked at him and thought of Derek.

Did you feel guilty?

I suppose I did. Anyway, he said you didn't want me to phone.

That's right.

You don't want me to go now, do you?

No.

That's good, because I don't want to go. It took a lot to get me to do this and I only did it because it's important. I wanted to speak to you. Why didn't you want me to phone?

I wasn't sure I'd have anything worth saying. We could talk like this forever. It's about as much as we ever did. But I'm not sure we could talk about anything else.

She muttered something; I'm not sure what it was, more like a sound than a word or phrase, like a sigh. And because I thought she was going to say something, I didn't speak. There was more I could have said, wanted to say, but I was waiting for her and she didn't speak, which created a space that went on too long.

I asked if it was difficult getting around London, knowing how long it takes to go from one place to the other and how I always went by tube because I could handle that system more easily than buses. And before there was time to create another space, I asked if she was seeing Alan.

I never was seeing Alan, not that way, not the way I think you mean. It had been going on, I told you that, but by the time I met you it was over.

Derek thought you were seeing him.

He always thought there was something going on. He couldn't work out what I was doing away from him. He always thought I was with someone else.

And you weren't?

Not at first and not for a long time and even then not the way you mean.

Did you tell him?

He wouldn't believe me because I spent time away.

Why?

I couldn't stay with him. I used to walk around Glasgow, go to the cinema, buy a book, sit in cafés and read, go to the library; anything rather than go home. And the reason I didn't want to go home was because I never knew how he'd be. Some times he'd be fine, other times he'd be blitzed and when he wasn't blitzed he was angry, or else he wouldn't be there. I keep thinking there was more I could have done, should have done, but I didn't do it and I didn't do it because I couldn't. I just couldn't do it.

If you did the best you could there's no reason to feel guilty.

You don't understand.

I'm trying to understand—

She screamed down the phone. I felt a sharp pain in my ear and pulled the phone away, when I came back she was sobbing and spoke between tears.

I did what I could. But it wasn't enough. It was never

enough. Or I wasn't good enough at it. I tried drinking with him. I tried drinking what he drank, but I got sick. I'd get sleepy and waken absolutely ill. I did all sorts of things to try to get him to stay at home. I bought drink for him, I'd try to control the amount he drank and I'd get up in the middle of the night and pour the stuff down the sink. I took money out his pockets and went round the house looking for the places where he'd hidden drink. And don't tell me to go for help. I tried that. I went to meetings and all I heard were people saying I should let go, let him go, let him get on with it, live a life for myself. But I didn't know how. So, it was either that or listening to women who hid their husband's clothes.

There was a long pause while she cried. Everything I thought of saying sounded lame and just when I thought I would have to speak, she blew her nose and sighed.

And he said horrible things; terrible, wicked things. He'd call me ugly and stupid and that was the beginning. You can guess the rest. And he'd go on and on about my mother, what she was like and how she didn't like him and had never liked him and when I pointed out she had given us money, especially when we were nearly thrown out because he told me he'd paid the rent but drank it and when he didn't pay the council tax and had credit card debts the length of your arm. He forgot she paid for our holidays. He said these were the things that made her despise him. And, of course, he'd get violent. He was a bully, that's what he was a big bully who'd throw his weight around when he was drunk and forget about it in the morning or would run away because he couldn't face me or would come crawling, literally on his hands and knees, begging me to forgive him, not to go, this was it, this time he'd quit, this time, he swore on his mother's life he'd stop. I had an abortion because of him and I lost a baby. He punched me and I fell downstairs. No wonder he didn't want to write stuff. And don't keep saying sorry. It isn't your fault.

But I am sorry. I'm sorry you had to go through this.

Me too. And I'm even sorrier I didn't do anything about it. And don't, please, please don't tell me I didn't fail, that I did what I could and it was up to him. His decision. I know that. But it doesn't make things better. No wonder I'm on medication. No wonder I'm fucked up. Do you know, he could never remember the horrible things he said and did, or he said he couldn't. I almost got to believing him. And don't, please don't give me an explanation. I've heard it all. Doesn't make it better. Nothing, nothing makes it better. I went to the doctor, told him what happened, told him I was paranoid. A misnomer, he said. There are lots of misnomers. He told me his job was to explain things, to demystify the process. I told him about Derek and he told me I was depressed, clinically depressed. It will come as no surprise that I'm on medication, quite a heavy dose. I've been on it for some time. I wanted to come off and he advised against it. Everybody feels like this he said. It isn't you. Everybody feels they've lost out some time or another. Everybody feels disappointment. Anyway, what's the point of this? I phoned because I thought I'd like to see you. I thought we might have something in common and I thought you'd make me feel better. I thought we might go and see Derek, actually face him. But this has been all too upsetting, and I'm sorry I bothered you.

Did you tell Alan about the back money?

What back money?

The money Derek was supposedly due for working for Alan. Was it your idea?

I could hear her grip the phone.

One final thing, is the house sold?

She hung up.

Nothing settled. I stared across the city, watching the planes come and go. I tried to work, spoke to people and tried to listen. I got in the car and stared at the road, or I drove nowhere, music blaring. I went to the supermarket and bought food I couldn't be bothered cooking.

I went to bed exhausted, wakened three hours later and sat by the window as dawn streaked the city sky. The nights seemed to have grown shorter without me, the weather strange and unpredictable, ice and sunshine, rain and mist in the same day. I'd walk through the park in the twilight that came around five, watching the occasional rocket and the descending trail of coloured light.

Jennifer's mobile was switched to voicemail. I didn't leave a message.

I tried handing out soup and talking to punters. I volunteered for extra duties, night manager at a hostel, driving the van, sorting clothes, that sort of thing.

After maybe three or four weeks I looked up Alan's office number. Can you tell me how to get in touch with Jennifer? I asked him.

Phone her.

I've tried. No luck.

Then go to The Bank.

Sorry?

It's a pub. She's there most nights after work.

Where is it?

How the hell should I know? I don't go. More your line of territory I would have thought.

She's still in Glasgow then?

Didn't go to London, came here asking for her job back. I put her in touch with someone and she's still around. Don't know where she's staying or what's going on, just that she's part of The Bank crowd. And I only know that because I asked, same as you.

The old wooden counter was used as a bar. They still had the black and white marble floor, the ornate ceiling and pillars, which were brightly painted and lit. There were brass chandeliers with huge globes and small tables and chairs near the windows.

She was standing at the far end of the bar, talking with three men, drinking mineral water. I didn't recognise her at first. I came in, looked around and, when I didn't see her, turned to go. Then I thought I saw her, but her hair was different, shorter, and streaked.

She looked wonderful, almost radiant, enjoying the attention. I sat at a table and watched as she flirted with all three men simultaneously. She wasn't the only woman in the place. There were others in similar groups, interspersed by light posses of men. This was where they met people like themselves.

The ambiance became obvious when a stranger, an attractive dark-haired woman, stood in the middle of the room, looked around and made her way past the bar, where most of the men tried to catch her eye, or stared at her back as she passed. She was obviously uncomfortable and glad to reach the restaurant.

Jennifer, in the meantime, had gathered her stuff. When the barman shouted, Taxi, she and one of the men, wearing a striped suit and shirt, a spotted tie and carrying some papers, walked past me, her arm in his.

I left, looked in at a meeting then went home through the park alone.

My strongest memory is something I never saw, Derek's mother taking a taxi to visit her son, to sit by his bed and expect a recovery.

That was the end and I knew it.

It was impossible to stay detached, impossible not to grieve, for them and the people they affected, for me and my half-life, trying to live between what I had and what I wanted, trying to hold on and let go, trying to stay detached because to be involved means accepting the unknown.

For a while I wished I'd been braver, had followed my feelings instead of my head. Then I knew what I was thundering about. I wanted another chance. I wanted to do what could not be done. I wanted to try again, to try and try and keep on trying till I got it right, to never give in.

I swore if I got that chance I'd take it, swore I would grab it with both hands, hold it close and never let go; to take it, take it all, take everything, then pay for it.

Someone other than who I was

Mrs Russell put her bag on the table and switched on the kettle before checking if there was enough water.

My cats, she said, as an apology and sat on the edge of the group.

Tom had been reading from his novel about a soldier with Robert the Bruce's army.

Seems a good point to interrupt, said Dave, looking up for my approval. I nodded.

Who gives a fuck about Robert the Bruce anyway? he said. Maybe I've grasped the wrong end of the thistle, but I don't think your average punter's too bothered about Robert the Bruce.

Then it's up to me to make them. And you have got it wrong. The book isn't about Robert the Bruce.

Aye, well, okay, maybe no Robert the Bruce, but the point I'm making is that historical fiction is, by its very definition, unreal.

His comments were addressed to Karen, who was staring at the floor.

Have you finished swearing? asked Mrs Russell.

Don't tell me you're going to start.

It was a question. And I very much doubt if anyone could tell you anything.

Was that the end of a chapter? I asked.

I'm not doing chapters, just sections. I think it's more impressionistic.

Can I have some comments?

It's very good, said Betty, who nodded while Tom was reading.

Dave sighed. Aye, well, it's good right enough, for what it

is. But it seems to me the question is not what it is, but what it could be. What do you think, Karen?

I think it's interesting. I don't know much about history, but hearing something like that makes it come alive.

Anyone else? I asked. Or can we move on?

Could you do mine? said Mr Anderson.

Mrs Russell sighed. The kettle's boiled, she said.

Other people have to read, said Mr Anderson. I'll do my piece.

Telephone banking is a fad and further evidence of the way standards are slipping in today's banking world. To my mind, nothing can replace the cheery teller who knew you and who was part of the same community as yourself. Cash machines and telephone banks may be part of today's society, but, just as junk food is replacing "halesome fairin", and if scientists are to be believed we are paying the cost in obesity and anti-social behaviour and folk are having to be taught to make soup and eat salad, then society will surely come to rue the day it closed the local bank and replaced the ledger with the computer.

Were you made redundant when your branch closed? asked Dave.

I was happy to take early retirement.

Mrs Russell was staring at the floor. She looked away when Mr Anderson asked for comments.

It's very good, said Betty. Makes you think.

And what about you? he asked. Would you like to comment?

I stopped listening, said Mrs Russell. It was very boring.

Are you German? he asked.

You've asked before and I've told you. I'm from Yugoslavia, which no longer exists.

I thought you were German because you cannot pronounce the letter *r*. My wife and I have had many happy holidays in Austria. The Tyrol is lovely. Still, if you are not from here you won't be familiar with the issues raised in the letter, will you? And what about you Tom?

Fine, sure, yeah, great.

What does that mean? Did you like it?

Yes. It was very good.

And what about the teacher?

It seems to me that with a little time and thought it could easily be developed into a short article. There's a touch of reminiscence, which could be expanded; you know the sort of thing, local branch, high counters, open fires, all of that. But I don't think it's publishable as it stands.

You said that before and the letter was published. In fact, the editor thought it was very good and asked for another letter. I mean, it's only your opinion.

Which is what you asked for and if that's not what you want you'll have to ask yourself why you're here.

Betty read three verses of a poem on how she felt when she looked at her granddaughter, wondering if the child would remember her.

What do you think, Dave?

Yeah, well, it's very interesting.

What's interesting about it?

The fact that she's tried to articulate what she feels.

And why should that be interesting?

Maybe Tom could tell us if he likes it?

I wouldn't like to interrupt your train of thought.

I asked my husband what he thought and he said he liked it very much, said Betty. Dave's right. I tried to express what I felt and I'm glad that comes across.

Yes, said Dave. Of course it does. How does that sound to you, Karen?

I liked it. I understood it. I'm not a grandmother, but I am a mother and I can understand she would feel these things about a baby.

She isn't a baby. She's nearly three.

But surely everyone feels these things.

Of course, said Mrs Russell. What you are avoiding is that

this isn't a poem at all. It has no form and very little content. It is sentimental and embarrassing. Why come here if you only want to hear everything's fine? Don't you want to improve? Surely you don't want to keep on producing the same standard all the time. Surely you want others to think you are capable of doing more.

We never hear you read anything, do we?

I must agree, said Mr Anderson. I find your comments distinctly unhelpful, given the fact that you don't contribute anything yourself.

I believe in telling the truth, she said. But you wouldn't understand that.

Two weeks later the librarian gave me an envelope.

Isn't she coming back then? Tom asked.

I'm not sure. I'll read this and get in touch.

I have a new poem, said Betty. And I've started a story. Perhaps you'd like to read it. It's just a page.

We'll do it when it's finished.

I'd like to read an article I've done for the local paper, said Mr Anderson. It's about fishing. It's called *The One That Got Away* and I've handed it in.

I'm thinking of writing a novel, Mrs Clark told Tom. This was her second class. She'd told Dave to wash his mouth out. He told her to fuck off and hadn't been back. Karen phoned to say she wouldn't be at the class: babysitters.

Has anyone else brought work? I asked.

I've had a letter from a publisher saying they've accepted the manuscript, said Mrs Clark.

Do you mean received?

It's very expensive, sending it round like that. Is there no other way? Perhaps you could send it to your publisher. I'd let you read it.

I think we should start, said Betty. I'll do my poem. It's called 'A Rose'.

Mrs Russell used a manual typewriter and single spacing. The page numbers were written in blue ballpoint on the top right corner. She had added sentences down the side of the page with postscripts and additions on the back of receipts and handouts. There was often little or no connection between the paragraphs.

What difference does it make? I married him. He was happy. I got his name and a passport and he got me.

I wanted to be someone other than who I was. And now I am Mrs Russell, though I am also what I have been. How can I tell who I was and what I became? I would have to lessen the story, would have to make it happen to someone else to make it believable, yet it happened to me.

And I knew; from the time they came into the courtyard, I knew. The tall one who never spoke, looked at me and grabbed my dog, Mitzi, a small dog, silly and always barking when she wanted to play. I said, 'Quiet, Mitzi.' But she kept barking.

He bent down and stroked her and when she started jumping as if to play he held her by the skin at the back of her neck, held her in the air like a sack, took out his gun and shot her head off. Then he looked at me and I knew. He was holding the body of the dead dog and his arm, his clothes and the side of his face were covered in blood. The others laughed. But he did not laugh. He looked at me and I knew, knew not to cry or to let him see it affected me in any way.

Even when they held me down in the yard, two men kneeling on my arms, two holding my legs and one on top, changing places, taking turns, even then I didn't cry.

Karen said, I need to see you.

She was dark-eyed and tall with narrow shoulders and long legs. I liked the way she always looked neat and straight, almost regal. She never wore make-up and her skin had a slightly tanned appearance.

It is not unknown for people in my position to have affairs with folk who come to the class and I wondered about me and Karen, walking through a silvery rain in the spring sunshine. She was waiting when I arrived. She looked untidy, drawn and tense and started talking immediately.

I have to tell you what's happened, not because I'm frightened or ashamed, but because I have to tell someone and you're the only person I trust who knows us both. Did you know I'd broken up with Benji's dad? I told Dave what happened, one night after the class we went for a drink. I saw him a bit later and he's written it up as a story.

Robert the Bruce's soldier had fallen for a beggar girl and was dreaming of a future, though he was disappointed when he saw the Bruce, who was small, bald and fat.

I don't know what to do with him, said Tom. I feel there should be more to him, something that seems more typical of his time. I don't feel he's real enough. Something needs to happen to make him more realistic.

Mrs Clark's novel had been rejected, but she'd heard from a magazine: If I rewrite the story they'll publish it, she said.

And a poem had been accepted for an anthology she'd seen advertised in a women's magazine. Copies of the book cost £35.00. Does anyone want to buy it? she asked.

Mr Anderson had written *How Lucky We Are To Have Local Libraries*.

However, he said, I have something far more interesting.

I've seen this, said Tom. I know what it is and I don't think it has any place here. It has nothing to do with this class.

I beg to differ. I think it has everything to do with the class. So much so that I have taken liberty of photocopying it.

Tom gathered his stuff.

This concerns someone who used to come to the class, he said, and is no more than a series of allegations. You've no right bringing it here and it's difficult to think you've done this out of anything other than malice.

A Sunday newspaper reported that the Bosnian authorities had applied to the British government for Mrs Russell to be extradited to face charges brought by a new state prosecutor. A commentator said there was a strong political element: the government was in economic difficulties and this could divert attention and go some way in restoring a sense of national unity. At best, it was a diversionary tactic.

The story alleged that as Dijana Dizdarevic in 1993, in the municipality of Konjic in Bosnia and Herzegovina, Mrs Russell had taken part in the massacre of 22 Croat civilians and eight prisoners of war. She and five other members of the Zulfikar special unit of the Bosnian army carried out the attack. The victims were killed by firing squad and she had been identified from photographs.

The article said Mrs Russell was a Muslim, that she lost several members of her family in the conflict and was the victim of a wartime rape. She was willing to testify against the other participants, to provide the court with all information and evidence relating to the attack and had expressed remorse to the relatives of the victims.

The matter was in the hands of the Foreign Office where no one was available for comment, though it was expected she would be extradited.

I arrived after midnight. I thought of putting a packet of cigarettes through the letterbox and leaving a bottle of wine on the doorstep, but if reporters had been hanging around, it could have given the wrong impression.

The house was dark. When I knocked, I thought I heard a movement behind the door.

It's me, I said. Mrs Russell, it's me.

She lived in a basement that seemed darker than the street.

It took time to adjust to the low ceiling and dim light bulb struggling against the confusion and the smell.

Excuse the mess, she said. My cats.

There was a small sitting room with a sofa and a blanket of coloured crocheted squares over the back.

She brought through a tea plate with salad and a hard-boiled egg in slices. We ate facing each other with the plates on our knees, drinking from a bottle of pale red wine.

The lamp and gas fire were the only lights in the room. I was aware of a bookcase at my back and a dresser to the left. Her chair was beside the fire, facing the television.

She had known for some time, sent everything she had to the judge who was handling the case and had still to hear about her extradition. The paper told her they were running the story and asked for a comment.

At first, the phone barely stopped ringing, but the people outside had gone away. Now there are calls during the night, at three and four in the morning. No one from the Foreign Office had been in touch.

I take it the story's true?

What difference does it make? We did what we had to do to survive. Everyone is guilty. If this story is true, am I more or less guilty than the woman who gave her daughter to the soldiers, who sold her body for nylon stockings or chocolate bars, the men who dug the pits or the boy who drove a wagon, knowing what was in it, the thousands who say they never saw or heard, the people who looked the other way?

She drank as she talked. Twice she finished a bottle and came back with another, pouring a drink when her glass was empty, tilting the bottle in my direction. She drank at least twice as much as me and seemed to smoke continually. Her voice was low and flat, deliberate, as though she was reciting something she had been forced to learn.

It sounds silly, she said. It's no defence, not really. But I cannot remember what I was like when I was a teenager.

Who can? Do we not do things then of which we are later ashamed, especially women? Do we let them overtake us? Do we sit and mope and continually make amends. What about you, have you led a blameless life?

I've never murdered anybody.

Then you are very fortunate. Do you, does anyone think I walked away unharmed? I ignored the pleas of the men who got down on their knees in front of me, I heard the children's screams and have tried to obliterate them, but nothing works.

You're not seriously suggesting you had no choice, that you're a victim?

No. I made choices that were based on my opinions and experience, on my greed and ambition, like everyone else. I knew what I was doing and I believed in the things I did, otherwise I couldn't have done them. And seeing it now, looking back, I don't blame anyone else; I'm not saying I was innocent. I am saying I was wrong. Part of me hopes they kill me. But they won't. They'll send me to prison and rehabilitate me. I don't care and I've never cared. They say I've been dehumanised and perhaps they are right.

By now she was drunk. She slept, suddenly waking and staring at me, then lapsing back to sleep. I sat for a while, listening as she dreamed and muttered in a language I did not recognise.

I put the crocheted blanket round her, turned off the fire and the light and walked home, thinking of the small clump of daffodils and bluebells that bloomed every spring by the side of the A85 to Oban. I first saw them as a child and looked for them every time I passed. The house had gone, but the daffodils remained, blooming every year.

Dave brought a story.

I wondered if you'd take a look, he said.

Run up a few copies and we'll do it in class.

You might want to look at it first.

No need. We'll do it in class.

Mr Anderson was about to read his article on recycling when Karen arrived. Her skin was shining, slightly darker than usual and she'd put a little make-up round her eyes. The light caught her hair. She had a short dress below her raincoat and raised heels. She sat opposite Dave, smiled at me and crossed her legs.

It occurred to me that we used to throw out our rubbish, Mr Anderson said when his reading finished. Now we have to keep it.

It's very good, said Betty.

Yes. It seemed an unusual subject. Something I could get my teeth into. I like something like that, slightly unusual. Have you brought your story?

No, said Betty. I'm still working on it.

It would be good if you could do something slightly different.

I'm going to put a twist in the tale.

Very good. I'll look forward to hearing you read it.

Tom's soldier had been wounded at Bannockburn and taken to Inchcolm Priory. When his injuries healed he went to Stirling to find the girl, but no one had seen her. It took him five days to reach Edinburgh where he met her brother, who was working for an apothecary who had seen her with a soldier from Edward's camp heading across Minch Moor. She was probably in England.

It's very sad, said Betty.

I reckon people were pretty much the same then as we are now, said Tom. They did what we do and felt the same things.

Perhaps not so sophisticated, said Mr Anderson.

I don't think we're sophisticated, said Tom.

Mrs Clark had entered a competition called Memories. She brought a couple of poems and a story about the Fair Friday her father came home drunk, having lost his pay. The poems were about the people who lived beside her and the way the city had changed and how, walking down Buchanan Street, she remembered what used to be there.

I suppose we've all heard about Mrs Russell? Dave said to no one at the interval.

The matter's been fully investigated here, said Tom.

I followed the story fairly closely, Mr Anderson said, and it just faded. There was the Sunday thing, then the dailies picked it up, but it was dead by Wednesday. By the way, I don't know if anyone picked up on the fact that she was a Muslim.

Just shows you, said Dave. You never know.

Never know what?

You never know who you're dealing with.

There were no subtleties about her, Mr Anderson said. She was too direct, too anxious to hurt someone's feelings.

What happens if she comes back?

She won't come back, he said. She can't.

Why not?

Well, for one thing I expect she'll be sent back to where she came from and will spend some time in jail. Apart from that, she wouldn't be welcome.

Is that because she murdered people or because she didn't like your work?

Her opinions meant nothing to me. I simply don't want to associate with someone like that. But it isn't up to us to say whether she should be here or not. Surely it's up to the teacher.

I rather liked her, I said. I thought she livened things up a bit.

I'm not sure I understand what you mean, said Mr Anderson. Did you agree with what she said?

Not always, no; but some of the time, of course.

I agree, said Tom. I think Mr Anderson would like to shut her up because he didn't like what she said. Is it her past you object to?

It's a matter of conscience. We have to make a stand. She has to know we do not approve of what she did.

What makes you suppose she might think otherwise?

I'm sure she doesn't. But I don't think we should be seen as sympathisers.

Just because she comes to a writing class doesn't mean we sympathise with her views or approve of her past. She may have changed for all we know.

That would be convenient.

So whether she has changed or not, you still won't believe her. Isn't that a policy she might have supported?

You misunderstand me. I was thinking of writing about it, said Mr Anderson, putting my views on paper as a record. I think someone has to be clear.

What about you, Dave? I asked. Will you be putting your views on paper?

No.

Have you copied your story?

Are you going to read a story? asked Karen.

No, he said. It isn't finished. Not really. It's just a few notes.

What a shame, said Tom. We've waited so long. What's the story about?

It isn't finished.

Perhaps the atmosphere might be a bit hostile, said Karen, especially if you don't know what you're dealing with. If there's nothing else, no other work, I've got a story.

I'd like to hear it, said Mr Anderson.

Her voice was strong and confident. She faced Dave, glancing up every now and then, as though reading to him.

I invited Lily to stay for a few days. Brian phoned to ask if he could visit.

My boyfriend went off to see his friend who had a pub outside Arbroath. Or maybe it was when he had the pub in Aberdeen, the one that was supposedly haunted by the ghost of a workman who had died installing the service lift, who slammed doors and walked along the upstairs corridor.

I bought bottles of wine. They brought bottles of wine. Lily brought me flowers with a little card tucked inside: To my best friend xxx.

We drank the wine. Every so often, Lily and Brian would look directly at each other. When Lily went through to the kitchen to have a cigarette, Brian and I kissed. Lily came back through and started crying. I put my arms around her. She disappeared again and came back wearing a black silk camisole over her jeans. She was flat-chested, almost like a boy.

She'd slipped a strap down below her shoulder. I went to change into my pink silk teddy. The evening now seems like a series of events without a soundtrack. We went through to my bedroom. As the three of us slipped under the duvet, I thought of the mess of bottles and cigarette butts back in the living room. Brian lay on the left of the bed, Lily in the middle, me on the right. Lily and I kissed. I could feel her legs brushing against mine. They were bristly and I didn't want to touch them. Brian was irritated.

Are you just going to ignore me? he said.

Lily and I fumbled for a bit. Then a wave of utter loneliness swept over me. I turned over, my voice muffled by the pillow.

Go to the spare room. I want to sleep.

They left. I grabbed my large stuffed rabbit with the pink ribbon and cuddled into it. I think I cried for a bit, then fell asleep.

The next morning I got up about 10, hungover and puffy-eyed. The door of the spare room was closed. I made a lot of noise, slamming the door on my way out to get a Sunday paper, then clattering crockery when I got back and made myself a cup of tea.

The spare room stayed closed. I grabbed my keys and caught a bus into town, leaving the previous night's wreckage to be dealt with later.

When she finished, Tom was smiling. There was a stillness rather than silence, as though they were waiting for something that would allow them to continue.

Names have been changed to protect the guilty, Karen said. Or rather, one of the names has been changed. I don't know why. Couldn't really bring myself to write the guy's name.

Does anyone want to say anything?

I loved it, said Tom. And I wanted more. I don't really have anything else to say.

I'm not sure I found the subject suitable, said Mrs Clark.

I know what you mean, said Betty.

I mean, it was well enough written and all that, very compelling, but not what I want to hear. There's enough of that sort of thing on television, isn't there.

What does Mr Anderson think? asked Tom.

Well, it's another world, isn't it?

Not really. You have no views on loneliness and despair?

I don't think that's the sort of thing I want to hear. There's enough of it in the newspapers and, as Mrs Clark says, it's also on television. What does the teacher think?

I'd like to hear Dave's thoughts.

Yeah. It's good. It's the best thing she's written.

Do you want to do your story?

No, I'll leave it.

Tom and I went for a drink.

Wee celebration, he said. Finished the book, sent it off and now we wait and see what happens.

While working on another?

He smiled.

So you won't be back?

I don't think so. It got me started and made me think about what I wanted to do.

By the time I got home I'd decided to leave.

What are we going to do? said Betty.

We'll have to find someone else, said Mrs Clark.

I have a short piece, Mr Anderson said. Nothing important, of local interest only, perhaps you could do it before you go, since this is your last class. It's on immigration.

I don't think I've anything to say, I told him five minutes

later, other than to tell you with some relief that I disagree with every sentiment it both expresses and suggests. And it's what it suggests that's most disturbing.

I was wondering, he said. If we don't get a replacement tutor, could we send some of our stuff on to you, just for your own interest and perhaps you could write a comment or two on each piece.

That's a good idea, Mrs Clark said.

No. That won't be possible.

That night I read the opening halfdozen pages, finishing with how Dijana Dizdarevic became Anna Russell, the website, her husband's visit to Sarajevo, her marriage, his family's disapproval and, finally, divorce.

I'd always longed for a permanence I could believe in; even when I was miserable, I was afraid of losing what happiness I had. This week, next week some time soon, it would happen, the skies would open, the blight would come and I'd be struck. The only certainty was death, far more certain than God; and though I envied those who believed in God, I could neither accept nor understand their trust, far less throw my hopes upon uncertainty.

Next day I phoned. I tried at least three times in the following days and was eventually answered.

My name is Jackie, the voice said. I'm with the social work department. The previous tenant has given up the flat and we're clearing it for reletting.

I asked if there were papers.

Papers?

Like a manuscript?

We cleared everything out. We got rid of a lot of papers, and, to be honest, none of the furniture or bedding was worth keeping, so we dumped the lot.

Just before Christmas I met Karen in a department store.

Isn't this awful, she said. Christmas shopping. Why do we do it?

How are you?

Good. What about you? Do you still take that class?

No.

Is it still going on?

I've no idea. Are you thinking of going back? Have you been writing?

Not really. I only did that stuff for the class. I think I was going through a bad time, she said.

William John MacDonald

The Mother

He's usually back by one.

When he didn't come in, I phoned Peter.

He'll be fine, he said. He'll be getting a lift off Lachie John.

But Lachie's car passed without stopping, so I phoned again.

I'll have a look, he said.

The Brother

He was at the side of the road, two miles out of town and six miles from home. He was on a bend and at first I thought he'd been hit by a car, but when I saw his face I knew it was different. He'd taken a doing, a really bad doing. He was unconscious, lying in blood and vomit.

I was lucky. I got a signal and had some credit, so I phoned the ambulance and waited till the paramedics came.

The Paramedic

There wasn't a lot we could do. We took him to hospital and waited till the doctor came. She took one look at him and said, Glasgow. Right away.

I don't know how he was alive. I was afraid to look at his head. His skull was almost lying open. He must have been kicked, but it was more than once. I think they kept stamping on his head. And his eye was out. I've never seen anything like it and can't imagine how anyone could do that to another human being.

The Girlfriend

I know Billy MacDonald. His Mum works in the Co-op. I think his Dad was lost at sea, something like that, an accident. We were in the same class right through primary and secondary; he stayed on and I left. I heard he was going to university, but I don't know what happened.

I know there was a fight and they said it was Andy. He'd left the pub and I didn't know where he was; but he was in the house, sitting by the fire when I got in. I asked and he said no. But his shirt and jacket were soaked in blood and there was even blood on his boots.

Don't tell anyone, he said. Please don't tell anyone.

I don't need to tell anyone, I said. Everybody knows it was you.

The Driver

I usually give Billy a lift home right enough. But he was in a fight. I don't know what happened. But I heard he fancied Kelly Ann Mathieson. He must've said something to her for Andy wouldnae've done that unless he'd said something, even though he can be funny, mind.

Anyway, I never saw him and thought he must've gone to Wilma's party. He usually says, but I hardly spoke to him all night, so when I never saw him at the end I just went home. It was next day I heard.

The Boyfriend

I don't know. I don't remember what happened.

I was drunk and don't remember.

The Barman

Billy was drunk. He gets drunk most weekends, falls about the place but doesn't cause any bother. He gets drunk, sometimes he sings that country and western thing 'Crazy', then he sits and is quiet. He usually gets a lift off Lachie John.

I didn't think there'd be a problem. That happens up here, then they sort themselves out when they leave to go to university at the end of the summer, or they get a job in Glasgow or someplace. There's no work here. The fish farm. That's it.

The Barmaid

I did, I saw a bit of it. He was at the bar and he was talking to Kelly Ann, nothing in it, just talking. He asked if she wanted a drink and she said no. He asked how she was doing and she said fine and asked how he was and he said he was going to university in Glasgow.

Andy had been in bother at work. I don't know what for and Kelly Ann took the boss's side and said he was in the wrong, which everybody knew would be the case anyway.

Andy was sitting by the door, watching Billy and Kelly Ann and he followed Billy out when Billy went for a smoke.

I was over by the door, collecting glasses. Next thing, I heard Billy scream.

The Helicopter Pilot

The weather was bad. We couldn't get up there. The call came in the middle of the night, about twenty to four and it was well after ten when we got up there. A lovely run. Lovely. Up there in just over an hour and back to Glasgow in the same time, maybe a wee bit more because a wind got up, but the sun was lying low over the water. Magical. Imagine living there and waking up to that every morning. It's a dream really.

The Barmaid

Billy did nothing to defend himself.

He went outside for a smoke.

I said something about him getting cheap fags because his mother worked in the Co-op and he said she didn't even know he smoked.

Then Andy came out. Billy was lighting a fag and Andy said, What the fuck were you saying to her?

Billy said, What? Saying what to who?

And that seemed to rile Andy. Saying what to who, he said. Saying what to who. Do you think I'm fucken daft.

He had something in his hand. It could have been a knife. I'm not sure, but he lashed out and the next thing Billy's let out this scream and put his hand up to his eye. Then Andy shoved him and started kicking into his head. Billy couldn't even defend himself because he was holding his eye.

They pulled Andy off, but he got away and jumped on Billy's head, fucken jumped on him with both feet, then jumped again. I don't know how many times he jumped on him.

Jesus.

We got him off and Billy was just lying there.

You stupid fucker, someone said. Get you to fuck out of here. Get off home.

Andy knew. He looked at Billy and he knew. He never said a word, never even went back into the pub, just went off home, ran down the road. It was the last thing I saw, him running down the road like a wee boy.

The Driver

I'll tell you what I heard. They took Billy and left him at the side of the road.

As if we didn't know.

As if anything's a secret here.

I think they thought the police would think a car had hit him.

I don't know for sure, but I can well imagine who did it.

The Mother

They told me Billy'd had an accident and I said what kind of accident and they said he's had a bad accident and he's in the hospital. Our Peter had told me they'd found him and he was in an awful state, so we went down to the hospital, but they wouldn't let me see him.

I spoke with the doctor, just a girl really, and she told me he was going to Glasgow and I could go in the helicopter with him if I wanted, but I asked how would I get back and she said she wasn't sure, so I said would I be able to phone Glasgow and she said she'd be sure to let me know what happens and she'd give me the number.

So I just waited.

The Police Sergeant

The paramedics have to tell us and we investigated. Waste of time. We knew what happened; but if you ask anybody, they saw nothing and heard nothing. We spoke to Kelly Ann Mathieson, Andrew MacLeod and Lachlan John MacKinnon and they all said they knew nothing. We spoke to the barman, Michael Smith, and the barmaid, Sarah Ann Campbell. She said nothing, though we know she saw what was going on, and she more or less confirmed what we already knew.

We could tell MacLeod was lying. Anybody could tell.

People saw you leave the bar after Billy.

I went for a piss, he said.

Who saw you in the lavatory?

And he just looked at us and said, Nobody.

The case is still open and will be open for some time. It'll come out. We know what happens up here. It'll come out.

The Doctor

No matter how many times you see this, you never get used to it. I got the call around half ten on the Sunday. I was told a serious case was coming in from the north and to get ready. It was an emergency.

I asked for the notes and there weren't any. They come with the patient, so I phoned the local doctor. She told me what I needed to know. A fight, severe fracture, internal bleeding, brain probably pierced with skull bone, eye almost certainly lost, cuts to the face and the paramedics had done a good job. No idea how long he'd been lying out on the road, but he had definitely been moved and could have lost consciousness when they moved him and after that he just drifted off.

I had the theatre ready; the anesthetist and nurses were waiting. They wheeled him in and I opened his eye to see if there was any sign and of course there was none, but there was something about the boy, the look on his face, or maybe just the face itself, a soft face, a sensitive face. It could have been an intelligent face. There was certainly no harm in it.

I don't often do that and I don't know why I did it then. I don't do it because I was advised not to; it can distract you, personalises the thing, makes it a person rather than a patient. But I'm not sorry I did it. He looked as if he'd been a nice lad.

I did what I could, of course. Things might have been different if we'd got to him sooner, but that's always the case.

The Mother

I don't know how I heard about Andrew MacLeod. But it didn't take long.

Billy was hit on the Saturday and I heard on the Monday.

Tell the truth, I didn't know how I heard, but when he came

in for cigarettes I told him.

My Billy's in hospital in Glasgow, I said. Do you know anything about it?

He never spoke, never said anything. Just looked at me and walked out.

The Nurse

We do everything for William. Three years he's been here, we wash and dress and change him, we feed him and try to give him exercises, move his arms and legs, sometimes we try and speak to him.

Sometimes he might respond to music. If a tune or a song comes on, country and western usually, you see something like a smile, as if he's trying to smile.

The Brother

It's done something to her. I don't know what it is, but I can see it.

Ever since my Dad died and I got married, Billy was everything to her. And since his accident, what else can you call it, she's taken on a new lease of life, a new spirit, as if she's fighting to bring him back, as if somehow doing what she does will restore him.

It's sad, such a shame. What can you do?

The Local Doctor

You never know, difficult to say. I've seen them survive if they're left alone. The kicking was the cause, but him being moved probably did more damage. He'd been put in a van and driven and left at the side of the road like a dead dog. Moving him could well have been as bad as kicking him, worse maybe. You can't tell one from the other. No one's to blame and they're all to blame.

The Mother

My Billy still can't talk, I told him. He was going to university and now he can't talk.

He never came back.

So I told her, the Kelly Ann one. I told her. You can tell that useless waster who sleeps with you that my Billy still can't talk. I hope what happened to my child never happens to your child, even though he's the father.

She stopped coming in as well.

So I told his father and mother and her father and mother and none of them said anything. Enjoy your grandchild, I said to them. I hope he's happy and well and a clever baby and I hope nothing happens to him like what happened to my Billy.

I put up a poster, reward for information leading to the conviction of the person or persons who harmed William John MacDonald. No response. Not yet.

None of them come in now. They've a round trip of more than eighty miles for their shopping. I was told to stop driving customers away and I told them I'm not driving customers away. They're perfectly free to come and go as they please. I'm only making conversation.

I hear he's going to Glasgow. But I'll find him. I go to Glasgow to see Billy and I'll find him when I go there.

It won't take long. Somebody's sure to know Kelly Ann.

The Police Sergeant

Not much more we could do.

It's an awful thing to say, but if the laddie dies and it becomes a murder inquiry, everything's different then.

We can subpoena witnesses, bring them in for questioning and eventually the truth comes out. But while he's still alive, there's not much more we can do. At the moment it's just an accident, a fight and there's plenty of them to investigate.

The Nurse

It's his Mum I feel sorry for. She's a lovely woman, always cheery and she comes down here as regular as clockwork. Mrs MacDonald's due today, we say without thinking.

There's no point in feeling sorry for William. His life is more or less over. But his Mum comes every two or three weeks. She brings crisps and sweets and juice and feeds him and she sits and holds his hand and strokes his hair and asks him to tell her who it was.

She brings new clothes for him, tracky bottoms and good shirts.

But he keeps putting on weight. He's over 20 stone now.

We tell her, Please stop feeding him rubbish. It's bad for him.

I have to do something, she said. I can't leave him like this.

The crossing

It's half past seven in the morning and she has been travelling for 18 hours. She left the baby with her mum, got the bus to Larne, boat to Stranraer and bus to Glasgow. She saved for weeks to make the trip, but had to borrow the last bit.

She has no idea how much she owes her mother, hundreds, maybe even thousands. Bits and pieces, the odd ten or twenty she'll never pay back and her mother never asks, but it's a worry. They used to go through a ritual where her mother would ask what the money was for and she always made something up, shoes, a school jumper, a nice dress she saw in a charity shop. Now she's down to essentials, the gas bill, dinner, bus fares. At first her mother said, Get something nice for yourself, knowing it would go on the wean, but now she asks, How much do you want?

There was no bother this time, as if she knew what it was for, as if she approved, though she would have given her nothing if she knew what it was for.

I see that wee Gerard Burns is on his own again, her mother said when she put the notes on the table. She, whatever her name is, was never right for him. I'd say he'd still be interested.

He took me to a dance when we were at school.

Still. You never know. Is that other one of yours, him with the belly, is he still around?

She thinks the boyfriend's the father, but she can't be sure. Her mother wouldn't talk to him and when he left she came round and squirted air freshener all over the place. But she still sees him, usually once a week and has to tell her mother she's doing something else.

There was a party. He got drunk and when they got home he went for her because she was talking with Gerry Burns.

You looked happy, he said, as if you wanted to be with him.

She was lucky. It wasn't too bad, not like the last time, but there's still a couple of bruises. She got away, ran when he was out in the street arguing with the upstairs neighbour.

It was raining, she'd nowhere to go and went back to the party. Brian Donnelly asked if she was all right and she said fine, took the glass he was drinking, swallowed it whole and danced with Gerry Burns. Then she was sick and passed out and wakened up in bed in his house. He was in the kitchen.

She dressed and was about to run out the door when he appeared with the tea.

In case you're wondering, I slept on the sofa, he said.

She didn't know whether to believe him. He said he wanted to see her again and phoned a couple of times. Maybe she'll give him a call.

When she got back the boyfriend was crying and promised it would never happen again. But he'd said all that before and is back in his own place, so she might be able to let him down gradually.

The smell of the bus station café nearly makes her sick. She runs to the bathroom to douse her face. She'd ordered a bacon roll but now she can't look at it. The plate must have been cold, there's grease on the edge; but she'll have nothing else and it was quite dear, though the tea's weak, just a teabag in a pot.

The woman opposite has been looking out the windows as if she's expecting someone.

Excuse me. Do you know where the Queen Elizabeth University Hospital is?

You're a bit from home? the woman says. My granny was Irish, from Monaghan. Do you know it?

Not really.

Ireland's a big place, I suppose. Go down to Central Station. I think you get a bus from there.

She stands and a sudden wave of tiredness makes her sit back down again.

Are you all right?

Not really. I've been up all night, travelling.

Is it a friend?

Sorry?

You're going to see. Is it a friend that stays here?

She nods.

My sister.

She'll be pleased to see you.

She can't remember because she burned the papers, but there was something about not having anything to eat before the operation.

When she comes back from the toilet, the woman's gone. She was going to flush the bacon roll, but she'll ask the girl to give it to one of the poor souls she'll surely see begging.

She goes back to the table and stares at the people. She'll need to ask the way to Central Station.

When she feels a bit better, she finishes the tea and takes out the newspaper the doctor gave her.

She hasn't read it; she knows what it says. The doctor told her.

You'll have to travel. Scotland's easiest. I could help you arrange things with the hospital, but you'll have to travel. There's no way it could happen here. We could get the jail, the doctor said.

And turn the water

Andrew Robertson caught a flash of gold and in that moment knew what he had long suspected. The implications swept through him like a plough.

When he tried to tell Janet, he could not describe the certainty. All he could see were the bits on the periphery, the edges that seemed not to matter, as if there was a gap between the moment and his conclusion.

He stood in the kitchen, his ruddy complexion and freckled, bald head moving awkwardly as he twisted his way towards the subject. It is, he said, difficult to describe an epiphany.

Janet swirled butter round the pan, added milk to the scrambled eggs and turned to look at her husband. She had rarely seen him this animated and expected him to pace the kitchen. But he was still, his head moving, as if he had found a solution, a kind of peace.

He told her he was on his way back from hospital where Mr Connor from the red house at the back of Kilrositer Brae overlooking the Rona Woods asked, Will you pray for her? Please.

Andrew Robertson had gone into the small side room without knocking, thinking he could leave a tract by her bedside. Mrs Connor was sleeping, her body barely distinguishable beneath the covers. Mr Connor was standing by the window.

I don't know what I am going to do, he said. I don't know what I'll do without her. Thirty-seven years it's been.

And while Mrs Connor slept, Mr Connor closed his eyes and bowed his head while Andrew Robertson asked God to bless them, to give them His strength and help them pass through this difficult time.

Mr Connor shook his hand and thanked him.

Good luck, Andrew Robertson said. All the best.

And that was the turn, the start of it, the first infant kick.

What could I do? he said. Nothing. The woman was dying and I was helpless. All I could do was pray.

So what else happened?

Nothing happened. Not there. Nothing happened there. It's just that I saw a wonderful reflection, sun on the water and I wanted you to see it.

That's nice, she said, and smiled.

Andrew Robertson sat in the garden in the five minutes till tea was ready. He couldn't tell her. While he was talking he realised he could not conclude his discovery.

If it was true, if he had drawn the correct conclusion, his life and its work were pointless.

I'm useless. A twister, a quack and a wastrel, he said aloud, when Janet called.

They came from the city where he had been an assistant for nine years. They came after Gemma died. Neither he nor Janet could pass her school. Four months after the funeral, when they'd got back to talking, Janet said she had booked a holiday, nothing much just two or three days away in the car.

They stayed with Mrs McNulty at Craigdalton, sat in the garden and read, walked through Rona Woods and followed the path across the moor to the ring of stones that predated history. They found a cove and swam in the sea, danced at a ceilidh and on Sunday went to the morning service at Aberona, whose parish had been amalgamated with Craigdalton and Kilrositer.

He stood at the door and looked across Craigdalton Sound while Janet spoke to the minister's wife, and later in the kitchen she told them the drawbacks.

The manse was big and very draughty, but it was a lovely charge with maybe as many as twenty folk coming to the alternate churches. The main church was Kilrositer, a lively community with a lot of incomers, mostly folk from England with their own ways of doing things, but they needed a minister like everyone else. There was always something to do at the cottage hospital they were trying to save rather than have a round trip of more than eighty miles. All the churches were damp and cold, but very well kept and maintained by the kirk sessions.

What do you think? Janet asked on the way back.

It'll do us fine, he said. He's not leaving till the spring and things will have changed by then. We could make a fresh start.

She nodded.

He preached his last sermon in the middle of March and they had a reception where he introduced the new assistant, showed him round and received the parish's grateful thanks, cards, an album of photographs and a clock.

Things changed slowly over the next two years, windows were repaired, floorboards straightened and hinges mended. Two churches were painted, Cardinal red floor polish was applied to the Aberona entrance and a new porch light was fitted at Craigdalton. Janet started a magazine that covered all three parishes and on December 18 Christmas tree lights were switched on outside every church.

He did 19 baptisms, 16 marriages and conducted 24 funerals, the last on the weekend after Easter Sunday when he buried Mrs McNulty's granddaughter, who had meningitis. Her death had saved the cottage hospital, the sister said. It proved it was needed.

That night he watched Janet lift the lid to see if the potatoes were done while shaking her head at the wickedness of the news on the radio.

He thought of the policeman who came to the door when Gemma died, the young man beside him obviously stricken with a sudden desire to laugh because of embarrassment. And he thought of the service, of watching the kirk elders carry his daughter's body and later standing by her plot in the kirkyard, when Willie Anderson, the church officer, handed him the earth and he heard it rattle on her coffin.

That was when he knew it had changed. There may have

been a God at one time, but not any more.

His last sermon was on the importance of finding your own God, the one that suits you. Never mind what anyone else thinks, no matter what they believe, you have to find your own God in your own way, find a power you can believe in. If you believe He made heaven and earth and all that in there is, and it sustains you, helps you, sees you through your journey from one day to another, that's fine. If you only believe the creation miracles you can witness, flowers in spring, birdsong, sunset, that's fine too.

Janet spooned the peas and carrots on to the plate beside the stew and potatoes and they ate slowly, his mind on the girl, maybe 19 or 20. He'd noticed her when she came out the Co-op and ran across the road in the rain, her white blouse wet; he thought of the way her breasts shifted when she ran.

And on the Sunday coming back from Craigdalton he had seen the same girl raise her head towards a young man and smile, looking fully into his eyes.

She was the dead girl's sister. She had cried throughout the service and later thanked him, asking if he was new to the parish.

She looked up and smiled, then put her plate on top of his, the knives and forks in her left hand and asked him to repeat what he had said.

I think I'm invisible and I don't believe in God. I'm a fraud.

No you are not. You help others, people who do believe in God. You guide them through the small ceremonies that are important to them and they like and admire you for it. So do I, even more so since Gemma's death. As you well know, it strengthened my faith.

I can't see it that way. I saw something wonderful today. On my way back from the hospital, I saw the sun stretch itself across the sea and turn the water golden. The reflection caught me full in the face and dazzled me, made me close my eyes and for a moment I thought I might lose the road, but, obviously, I didn't, even though I kept looking at the moving sheet of gold that rippled as though it was alive, moving like a bird's wing. It was wonderful, an obvious act of creation, but I looked and stared and couldn't believe, not for the life of me.

Janet pressed his head to her breast. She kissed his brow and stroked the top of his head.

Later, he went into the garden after rain and smelled the earth and the conflagration of roses and honeysuckle, the night stock narcotic in the moonlight. He stood on the path and listened to the wind in the trees, the sough of the sea and thought of the calm on his dead daughter's face.

She's an angel, a woman behind him said.

Some of these stories in one form or another have been published elsewhere. 'Someone always robs the poor' appeared in *The Warwick Review*, 'Queen's Park' in *Causeway/Cabhsair*, 'Someone other than who I was' in *Gutter 14*, 'William John MacDonald' in *Gutter 5* and 'After the dance' in *Gutter 6*.

'Korsakoff's Psychosis' was written for John Murtagh and a few others, such as the Friday Team, who have nothing to learn from it.